Arou

Arousing Anna

Nina Sheridan

LIBRIS

An *X Libris* Book

First published by X Libris in 1995

A CIP catalogue for this book
is available from the British Library

ISBN 0 7515 1222 2

Photoset in North Wales by
Derek Doyle & Associates, Mold, Clwyd
Printed and bound in Great Britain by
Clays Ltd, St Ives plc

X Libris
A Division of
Little, Brown and Company (UK)
Brettenham House
Lancaster Place
London WC2E 7EN

Chapter One

ANNA CLOSED HER eyes on Paul's intent face as it hovered, inches from her own, and mentally navigated her way round Sainsbury's. They were out of self-raising flour and she must remember to buy some stock cubes.

She frowned, trying to concentrate on her shopping list as Paul began to breathe faster, in time with his by now frantic thrusting.

'Yes . . . yes, that's it . . . aargh!'

Opening her eyes, Anna saw that her husband's eyes were bulging from their sockets, staring fixedly at a point on the wrought-iron bedhead above her. This was her cue to rake her nails lightly across his shoulders, so, feeling obliging, she did so, throwing in a half-hearted groan for good measure.

'Ooh! Lovely!'

He rolled off her at last and she readjusted her nightie, mentally adding toothpaste to her shopping list.

'How was it for you?' Paul mumbled as usual.

Anna wondered why he ever bothered to ask since he was patently so uninterested, but she replied dutifully, 'Wonderful darling.'

Stifling a yawn, she turned over gratefully, glad to have the weekly grapple under the duvet over and done with. Lying awake in the darkness, she listened to Paul's heavy snores and wondered if this was it. Passion.

When she had married Paul, five years before, fresh out of her strict, sheltered boarding school, she couldn't wait for the formal reception to be over so that they could be alone and she could get his trousers off. She'd heard so much about Sin from the Reverend Mother, she couldn't wait to try it out for herself.

But, as tonight, she had ended up on her wedding night staring up into the darkness with a big, fat 'so what?' hanging over her head. A few perfunctory kisses followed by a flurry of uncomfortable, ineffective penile thrusts, and it had all been over. Paul, her handsome, longed-for husband had seemed happy enough, so Anna concluded – naively, she realised now – that it would get better with practice.

Later, when she finally plucked up enough courage to ask him about it, Paul explained that she simply wasn't the sort of woman who enjoyed making love. And when she tentatively hinted that she would like him to take more time, to help her discover all the joys of which she had read, he had let her know in no uncertain terms that, if she was unfulfilled, then the fault lay squarely with her.

Sometimes, just before Paul spilled his seed

into her passive body, she would get the most peculiar sensation, high in her womb. Once or twice she had tried to hang on to it, but it always receded, hovering just out of her grasp. And, if she dared to move beneath him, she suffered Paul's sulks for days afterwards.

Anna felt it tonight, that elusive tingle. If she squeezed her thighs together tightly, she could feel a pale imitation of it still.

Anna's sister, Leigh, had described the point of orgasm to her so graphically, so many times, she wondered if this might be its beginning. But no, it was receding again, leaving her feeling curiously empty. Just as she should feel, she supposed, if she was frigid, as Paul said.

She had only herself to blame, he sneered, if he liked to spend time with other, more responsive women. Though how she was supposed to respond, when he was so adamant that she shouldn't move so much as a muscle, was beyond Anna.

Leigh had other opinions; she said that no woman with an ounce of self-respect would put up with a philanderer like Paul. But then Leigh was a real, warm-blooded woman; she would always have alternatives. Whereas Anna . . . Anna clung desperately to the devil she knew!

Paul watched through half-closed eyes as Anna dressed the next morning. She crept about, careful not to wake him, her movements unconsciously graceful in the half light. A surge of irrational anger surged through his veins. God, why did she have to be such a bloody martyr?

He wasn't proud of the way he behaved, but there was something about Anna which irritated the hell out of him, making him want to kick her. Metaphorically, of course, he'd never raise his hand to her, he told himself hastily. He pushed away the uncomfortable realisation that emotionally, mentally, he abused her just as thoroughly as if he used physical violence.

He must have been a fool to marry her! He berated himself impotently as he watched her brushing her hair. That hair. So long and thick, it made her look so sickeningly vulnerable. And that lush, fertile figure, no angles or sharp edges about Anna, just soft, womanly curves and a gentle sweetness in her smile . . . It wasn't that he didn't love her, not really. He did in his way. But he knew now that he could never make her happy, any more than she could him.

Whatever had made him think that marriage to Anna would redeem him? All he had done was drag her down into his own pit of misery. Suddenly, he felt like crying. Balling his fists, he clenched them until his nails bit into the skin of his palms and the little pain made a man of him again.

Fully in control of himself now, he made a pretence of stretching and yawning, so that Anna would think he had just woken.

'Do you have to go to Edinburgh?' Anna despised herself for the plaintive note she could hear in her own voice as she watched Paul pack.

Irritation marred his bland good looks for a moment.

'It's only two nights, Anna. You've got that old French bloke coming to stay today, haven't you?'

She nodded and he shrugged carelessly, fastening the zip of his case with a finality which chilled her.

'Well then, it's not as if you'll be lonely, is it?'

He pecked her on the cheek and was through the bedroom door before she had a chance to argue.

'Be back by Thursday!' she called after him, knowing that two nights could so easily turn into two weeks. But her only answer was the slam of the front door behind him.

'I'm really not sure about having Monsieur Gérard to stay, Alan,' Anna told her boss even as they were on their way to the airport.

'Nonsense, Anna! I'd trust my own daughter with Dominic Gérard. He's a perfect gentleman and despite the reputation of the French, I assure you you'll find him very civilised. Even though your husband is away from home – again.'

Anna let the telling emphasis on the final word go without comment for, apart from being her employer at the University, Alan Sawyer and his wife, Sarah, were among her dearest friends. Infuriatingly, though, Alan never referred to Paul by name, always as *your husband*.

Anna sighed and gazed out of the window. The landscape began to flatten as they neared Heathrow and they were caught in the late afternoon commuter traffic.

There was no reason for her to feel apprehensive. She often played unofficial hostess to visiting dignitaries and generally she enjoyed it. It made her life as Secretary to the Head of Business Studies that much more interesting, and she was often glad of the company while Paul was away. As he frequently was.

'I'm sorry, I had no right to comment on your private life like that.'

Looking quizzically at Alan, Anna realised that he had misinterpreted her silence as disapproval. Smiling, she sought to reassure him.

'Nonsense! Besides, I don't take offence at friends.'

Alan looked relieved, his thin, intelligent face relaxing. He was a handsome man, even at sixty two. From the wedding photographs she had seen of him and Sarah, she knew that in his youth he had been quite devastatingly attractive. She felt a rush of affection for him and tried to explain her reluctance.

'You know I don't mind helping out, especially since Sarah has been so poorly. It's just that I've finally received an appointment from the Marriage Guidance people. It's next Thursday and I guess I feel a bit on edge.'

Alan's lips tightened, but he remained silent as he concentrated on navigating his way round the one-way system at the airport. Finally he said, 'If it's awkward for you, I could get Natasha to come home and help Sarah.'

Natasha was their daughter and Anna could not help but smile at the idea of the beautiful, affectionate, but totally unreliable creature helping Sarah to entertain the French businessman.

Alan caught her eye and grimaced. 'Okay,

perhaps that's not such a good idea. But really, if you'd rather not. . .'

Anna shook her head. 'It's all right, I'm being silly. Looking after Monsieur Gérard isn't really going to interfere with one, hour-long appointment with Relate. Anyway, it's only for a week, isn't it?'

Alan nodded and shot her a grateful smile. There was no more time for talking for they were by now parked and a glance at the digital clock above the driver's mirror told them that their guest would be disembarking at that very moment.

Anna stood next to Alan in the Arrivals Lounge and scanned the faces of the passengers streaming through. No one looked the remotest bit like one of the sweet old gentlemen who usually gave up their time to lecture on one of Alan's courses and she began to grow restless.

Her eye was caught by a tall, impeccably tailored man of about thirty who was talking animatedly to one of the airport staff, a young, dark-haired girl, impossibly pretty in her neat airline uniform. He did not seem to be in any hurry to come through the gate and Anna was fascinated to watch how he appeared to be saying as much with his hands as with his mouth. Even from that distance, she could see his fingers were long and elegant, like those of an artist. A sculptor, perhaps?

This uncharacteristically whimsical turn of her thoughts brought Anna up short and she tore her eyes away from the stranger impatiently.

'I wonder where Monsieur Gérard has got to?'

she murmured to Alan.

But Alan was not listening. He was holding up his hand and flapping it about in agitation.

'Dominic! Dominic – over here!'

Anna's jaw fell slack as the man she had been watching earlier turned at the sound of Alan's voice. She snapped her mouth shut as he said goodbye to the young girl and walked towards them.

As he approached, his features became clearer. His dark hair curled slightly round his ears and across his forehead. His face, lifted now by a warm, wide smile, was graced by the most extraordinarily symmetrical features.

Even while a part of Anna's mind registered amazement that she had noticed such details, she was aware of the most peculiar tightening of her abdominal muscles as he reached them, as if she had recently stepped out of a fast travelling elevator.

Swallowing hard, she stood by as Alan was enveloped in an exuberantly Gallic embrace. Then Alan stood aside and Anna was caught in the deep, chocolate brown gaze of her new house guest.

'Pleased to meet you,' she said awkwardly as Alan introduced her.

Her outstretched hand was taken in a firm but gentle handshake. She found herself incapable of looking away as he replied, in a voice like bristles over velvet, 'It is my pleasure, *madame*, and I am most grateful for your hospitality.'

His voice was thickly accented, but clear. Anna's eyes widened involuntarily as he swiftly lifted her hand to his mouth and brushed his lips lightly across her knuckles.

It was he who finally looked away and Anna found herself following the two men to Alan's car in a daze. As Dominic Gérard opened the rear door for her with a gallant flourish, Anna's arm brushed against his and she literally jumped back, as if the innocent, brief contact had hurt her.

Embarrassed, she forced a polite smile, her cheeks reddening as he raised a puzzled eyebrow. What is the matter with me? she asked herself as he closed the door and slipped into the front beside Alan. She was not generally known to be socially inept, yet here she was, acting like a gauche teenager with a crush on a man she had barely met. One thing was sure, if Dominic Gérard was going to spend the next week under her roof, she was going to have to overcome her ridiculous reaction to him – and quickly!

Time was getting on, so Alan took them straight to Anna's house, inviting them both to dine at his home once they had changed.

'Be casual!' he entreated as they reached the gate.

They exchanged a glance and Anna realised that her guest was as aware as she of Alan's deep-rooted horror of 'dressing up'. Anna opened the small, wrought-iron gate and ran up the steps to the house, searching for her key en route. Glancing over her shoulder, she saw that Monsieur Gérard had paused, his hand on the gate, and was looking up and down the wide, tree-lined avenue.

He turned and smiled at her and Anna felt

again that queer, sinking feeling in the pit of her stomach.

'This is a beautiful part of the country, with the leafy lanes, no?'

Anna smiled. 'I've often thought this area looks a little like the suburbs of Paris.'

He grinned and took the steps two at a time. 'Perhaps.'

'This way, *monsieur*,' Anna invited, as the old oak door swung closed behind them on its well oiled hinges.

'Dominic, please,' he protested as he followed her up the stairs, 'and your name is. . .?'

'Anna.'

'Ann-a,' he repeated, as if her name were some kind of puzzle he wanted to solve. The word seemed to slide across his tongue and Anna shivered inexplicably.

She showed him into the neat guest room. He dropped his suitcase on to the comfortable double bed and looked around approvingly. It was newly decorated in shades of blue and cream and Anna felt it looked smart rather than pretty. It was a masculine room, yet she had gone to great pains to ensure it was comfortable. The pale, cream carpet was thick and soft and the diamond patterned curtains at the window were gathered into generous folds.

That morning, she had placed a vase of fresh chrysanthemums on the window-sill and their cheerful yellow blooms lent the room a splash of bright colour. To her surprise, Dominic noticed them immediately and went over to touch them. Anna's eyes were drawn irresistibly to his hand as it cupped one of the perfectly formed flower heads and she shivered again as she recalled how it had felt in her own.

'Beautiful,' he breathed, his smiling eyes boring directly into hers.

Anna felt a warm glow of pleasure, far out of proportion to the small, implicit compliment made. To cover her confusion, she showed him the small en-suite bathroom. He nodded appreciatively, his sweeping gaze taking in the pile of thick navy and cream towels on the glass shelf and the toiletries she had provided, lined up neatly on the window-sill.

'You are very kind,' he smiled at her and Anna found her mouth had grown suddenly dry.

'There's plenty of hot water,' she burbled. 'Please feel free to take a shower before you change for dinner if you'd like one. We have an hour before we need to set off for the Sawyers'.'

She left him in the guest bedroom and went to see to her own clothes. From her bedroom, she could hear him moving about, presumably making use of the wardrobe and chests of drawers for she heard the sound of doors opening and closing. He must have unpacked quickly for she soon heard the shower running.

Glad she had had the forethought to bathe as soon as Paul left that morning, Anna washed and changed into fresh underwear before slipping into the dress she had laid out ready.

It was dark green, severely cut with gold buttons down the front and at the cuffs of the three-quarter length sleeves. Smoothing it over her hips, she cast a critical eye over her reflection and wished she had chosen something more attractive.

She brought herself up short. Why on earth would she want to make herself attractive to Dominic Gérard? God, you're pathetic! she derided her mirror image. Going all jelly-legged because some handsome Frenchman has paid you a compliment! You're a married woman, for heaven's sake. A neglected one, admittedly, but that's no excuse to behave like some sad, frustrated housewife!

It wasn't as if she was a particularly alluring woman anyway. She grimaced at herself in the mirror. As Paul so often pointed out, she was a little too broad in the beam to be worthy of a second glance and in this she had to agree with him.

Dominic, on the other hand, was worth a third and even a fourth glance when he found Anna in the sitting-room half an hour later. He had changed into taupe linen trousers and a navy blue blazer with a pale yellow turtleneck underneath.

'I thought you might like a drink before we leave?' Anna suggested hurriedly before he noticed her quick appraisal of him.

'Thank you. What are you having?'

'A dry sherry.'

'Then I'll join you, Anna, if I may?'

Again, there was that emphasis on the last syllable of her name which sent an inexplicable thrill through Anna's veins. She smiled tightly at him as she handed him his glass, taking care not to touch his fingers with hers. As he reached for it, she caught a waft of some subtle, spicy aftershave lotion, not sufficient to be over-powering, but enough to accentuate the tangy scent of clean, masculine skin.

Feeling slightly light-headed, Anna took the seat farthest away from him and tried not to watch as he folded his long, lean frame on to the sofa opposite. There was an awkward silence as they sipped their drinks.

'Have you lectured here before?'

'Have you worked for Alan long. . .?'

They laughed as they both spoke at once, dispelling the tension. Dominic shook his head.

'After you, Anna.'

Her question sounded even more inane a second time, but she repeated it anyway.

'I was just asking if you'd been here before?'

'In Surrey, no, but in England, many times. Luckily our wines are very popular here and I enjoy keeping in touch with our customers. Is this your husband?'

Anna was startled as he suddenly picked up the silver-framed photograph of Paul which stood on the side table. In it he was holding his coveted golf trophy, a smug grin stretching from ear to ear.

'Yes, that's Paul. He's away at the moment . . .' Anna blushed as she realised how her eagerness to explain his absence might be interpreted.

Dominic regarded her steadily, his brown eyes searching, before he replaced the photograph. Anna noticed that he had angled it slightly, so that she could no longer see it from where she sat.

'Perhaps we should start our journey?' he suggested smoothly.

Anna leapt to her feet and took Dominic's empty glass before fetching her bag and coat.

It was a warm evening, so she carried the coat over her arm as they walked to her car.

'No rain!' Dominic said, glancing upwards wryly.

'Well, it *is* June,' she reminded him.

The evening was far more enjoyable than Anna had anticipated it would be, given her embarrassing awkwardness around Dominic. Amongst friends, she began to relax and was delighted to find that she liked her guest more and more as she spent time with him.

It was obvious he was genuinely fond of Alan and Sarah and the older couple were easy in his company. Anna was touched by the tenderness he displayed towards the still frail Sarah. And slowly, so slowly she was barely aware of it, she began to uncoil, to forget the curious, inconvenient tension which had gripped her from the first moment of their meeting.

So that by the time they arrived back at the house, they were laughing happily together, comfortable with each other as if they were old friends, not acquaintances of a mere few hours duration.

As they entered the sitting-room, the toe of Anna's shoe caught on the edge of the rug and she half stumbled. Strong arms reached around her waist to steady her and she found herself brought up against Dominic's broad chest.

Somehow it seemed natural to turn in his arms and smile up at him. Anna sucked in her breath as she saw that his brown eyes had darkened and sobered, all humour gone now.

He's going to kiss me, she thought, and a part of her mind, the part that was still sane, even then, told her to move away now, while she still could. Too late, for his mouth was already on hers, moving gently, exploring, tasting, the tip of his tongue coaxing her startled lips apart.

Anna's eyes fluttered to a close as Dominic's hand tangled in her hair at the nape of her neck and the kiss deepened. She felt boneless, melting in his arms, aware of his every bone and sinew pressing against the length of her body.

It was several minutes before she realised that the ringing in her ears was not due to this assault on her senses, but to the telephone. Reluctantly tearing herself away, Anna crossed to the hall on shaky legs and picked up the receiver, aware of Dominic's dark eyes on her, watching her the whole time.

'H-hello?'

'Anna?'

The sound of her husband's voice on the other end of the line was like having a bucket of ice-cold water thrown over her.

'Paul? Is that you?'

She dragged the back of her hand guiltily over her swollen lips, her gaze colliding with Dominic's across the hallway. She felt a mixture of disappointment and relief when he quietly disappeared up the stairs, leaving her to deal with her call.

'Sorry? Did you just say you're staying on?'

'Yes, Anna – pay attention, can't you?' Paul sounded even more irritable than usual and Anna felt her heart sink.

'But Paul, you promised you'd come home on Thursday! We were going to go to Marriage Guidance, remember?'

'You'll just have to make another appointment.'

Anger and a familiar, impotent frustration surged through her veins.

'And have you break it again? Paul, we've waited months for this appointment. You know what the waiting list is like!'

The sigh on the other end of the telephone was thunderous.

'Go on your own then, if it's so bloody important. You're the one with the problem, after all.'

'Paul!' As usual she failed, miserably, to hide her hurt. She heard what sounded like a feminine giggle in the background.

'You're not alone, are you, Paul? You've got someone with you.'

He didn't even bother to deny it, though the tone of his voice was kinder.

'Look, I can't talk now. I'll see you in a month. If you want to keep that appointment so badly, go ahead. Get whatever therapy you need.'

Anna was left with the cold finality of the dialling tone. Crashing down the receiver, she ran up to her room, stopping herself just in time from slamming the door. Dominic was in his room – how much had he heard? Anna's cheeks burned with mortification, both at the idea that he might have heard her side of the conversation, and with the memory of the kiss they had shared.

Whatever mad genie had possessed her this evening, she was going to have to make it quite clear that she was not usually in the habit of being so friendly with her temporary guests! What explanation she could give for her uncharacteristic behaviour was beyond her. If her impatient, faithless husband could have seen her. . .!

Anna scowled at her reflection as she tissued off her make-up. The frigid wife he left behind would hardly throw herself at the first attractive man to cross her path!

Angrily plumping up her pillows, Anna rolled under the duvet and closed her eyes. But it was not the expected, dreaded images of Paul with his latest 'little adventure' which played behind her closed eyelids – rather it was the thought of the man who was sleeping a mere thin partition wall away and the memory of his lips on hers.

Chapter Two

IT WAS NO use, she wasn't going to be able to sleep. Restlessly, Anna pushed her feet into towelling mules and pulled on her old dressing gown. It was an old friend, that dressing gown. Faded now, it used to be pink, soft and fluffy and she would not part from it for all the slinky negligees in Lewis's. Quietly, so as not to disturb her guest, she crept downstairs to make herself some cocoa.

Preoccupied as she was with thoughts of Paul and the miserable sham their marriage had become, Anna was startled to turn round and find Dominic framed in the doorway.

He was wearing an impossibly white, thick towelling robe, his hands thrust into the deep pockets, out of sight. His strong, hair-roughened calves were bare beneath it, as were his feet and Anna wondered briefly if he was completely naked underneath. Feeling a hot flush of embarrassment seep up under her skin, she stammered, 'Oh! I-I'm sorry – did I wake you?'

He smiled and for the first time she noticed that his smile was crooked, slightly higher on the left side than the right, and that this small irregularity created a deep dimple in his left cheek. This minute imperfection in an otherwise perfect face seemed to enhance rather than detract from his wholly masculine beauty and for a moment she simply stared, fascinated, at his mouth.

'Anna?'

She started as he spoke her name, blushing even harder as she fancied that he could read her thoughts.

'I've just made cocoa – would you like some?'

He shook his head, leaning against the doorframe and watching her as she fumbled with the saucepan.

'I heard you come downstairs and I thought I would check that everything is all right.'

'Why shouldn't it be?' Anna bristled at his casual assumption that they were friends already and that he had the right to ask such a thing.

She looked at him in what she hoped was a suitably haughty fashion, but the feeling faded the moment their eyes met. He shrugged. How very French, she thought with sudden, unexpected amusement.

'You were upset by your husband's telephone call.'

It was a statement, not a question, but this time, curiously, she did not mind.

'Yes. I gather he plans to leave for Europe directly from Edinburgh rather than come home first.'

'It was important to you that he should come home?'

'Yes. We had a . . . an important appointment on Thursday. At least, I thought it was important . . .' Anna trailed off, conscious for the first time that her determination to save her marriage was not necessarily the only option open to her.

'And now. . .?'

She looked up as Dominic prompted her and smiled grimly.

'Now I think that perhaps the woman Paul is with is welcome to him!'

'Ah!'

Anna was surprised to find that admitting her hated 'wronged wife' status out loud was not as humiliating as she had anticipated. She felt her eyes widen as Dominic closed the distance between them and stood, inches away from her, scanning her face with enquiring eyes.

This close, Anna could see the hazel flecks near his pupils and the thick, double row of lashes framing his eyes. Even through the deep-piled towelling robe she could feel the healthy warmth emanating from his strong body and her own limbs began to feel heavy. The scent of his skin, clean, yet undeniably masculine, assaulted her nostrils and she found herself breathing in deeply, capturing it.

Dominic held her immobile with his eyes, his intense, brown gaze pinning her, stripping her bare as if he were trying to see into her very soul. So intent was his regard that Anna found herself holding her breath, her eyes suddenly leaden, half closing in languorous anticipation.

But he did not take her into his arms. Instead,

he raised one hand and placed the back of his knuckles gently against her cheek. Acting on instinct she turned her head, a mere fraction, so that she could feel his little finger against the corner of her mouth.

'Beautiful,' he whispered huskily, 'you are so beautiful, Anna. Your husband is a fool.'

And with that he turned abruptly on his heel and was gone. Anna stood for a moment, absolutely still, and listened to the sound of his footsteps as he went back up the stairs to his room overhead. Without the heat of his body to warm her, she felt cold. She shivered and hugged herself. Her untouched cocoa had congealed in the mug so she threw the disgusting concoction down the sink before making her way slowly upstairs.

Once safely in her room, Anna paused as she caught sight of her reflection in the mirrored doors of the wardrobe. Beautiful. It was not a word that she had ever thought to apply to herself, yet Dominic had sounded quite sincere. What was it that he saw that she, and indeed her husband, never did?

Anna tossed back her braid and stared at her reflection almost defiantly. The eyes gazing back at her were large, too big for her face and a nondescript grey. At least her nose was straight and nicely proportioned. She turned her attention to her mouth and tried not to twist it in self-mockery.

She had always been rather embarrassed by her mouth. It was wide and full-lipped, the lower lip slightly more protuberant than the other so that, in repose, she looked as if she had a permament pout. She knew it didn't suit her, that starlet's mouth, constantly promising something that its owner could not provide.

Tugging at the braid with which she habitually tied back her hair at night, she shook her head and let it fall about her face in deep, golden ripples. Secretly, she considered this her best feature. In the early days of their marriage, Paul periodically tried to persuade her to have it cut in a more modern style, but even he soon gave up. From when she was a tiny child, she had never had more than a levelling trim so it fell, when unrestrained, in luxuriant waves to below her waist. Like Goldilocks, Paul often mocked her.

Dominic, though, had never seen her hair other than when it was pulled back off her face, as tonight, or carefully rolled and pinned as she always wore it during the day, so she could not imagine that it was her hair that he found beautiful.

Taken up with her scrutiny of herself, Anna unbelted her dressing gown and threw it on to the bed. Her white, cotton lawn nightie concealed her body. Slowly, she pushed its wide straps off her narrow shoulders and, steadfastedly holding her own gaze in the mirror, she let it slide down her body to the floor. Without breaking eye contact with herself, she stepped out of it and kicked it to one side.

The still air of the bedroom felt chill as it enveloped her naked skin and she shivered. Her eyes reflected her nervousness and she smiled kindly at herself. Dragging her eyes away from their reflection, she let her gaze traverse the smooth, white skin of her throat, past the shadowy hollow at its base and down to the voluptuous swell of her breasts.

In the soft glow of the bedside lamp, her skin looked fragile, its surface pearlised. The pink areola surrounding the crown of each nipple looked tender, ripe like a soft fruit. Contact with the air had hardened her nipples so that they pointed provocatively at each twin in the mirror. Tentatively, Anna ran her hands along the underside of each breast, cupping them against her palms, testing their weight.

The ribs beneath looked too narrow to support them and she marvelled at the wonder of nature which allowed them to defy gravity and remain upright, proud.

Tracing a path down her sides with the flat of her hands, the sharp indentation of her waist pleased her and she ran one palm over the velvety soft skin of her belly, revelling in its womanly undulation.

Her hips flared gently from the narrow band of her waist and as she ran her hands across them, to the tops of her thighs, she realised for the first time that, far from being too large, her hips were in perfect proportion to the rest of her body.

Halfway down the outsides of her thighs, she paused and ran her eyes along the length of her legs and back up again, satisfied with what she saw. Her legs, like her hips, suited her body. They looked slim, athletic even, the subtly defined muscles long and strong.

Slowly, Anna smoothed her hands over the

fronts of her primly closed thighs, gently insinuating her fingers between them and gradually creeping up their smooth, firm length to their apex. Her fingers brushed against the silky, golden curls and traced their outline along her groin and across the base of the inverted triangle until they met, in line with her navel.

Deep within the crevice shielded from view by her pubic hair, Anna felt a stirring, a dampness which she longed to investigate. Her fingers fluttered downward, nearer to the small keyhole of light showing through her tightly pressed thighs and she felt a warmth seeping into her legs.

Anna jumped as another reflection joined hers in the mirror. Dominic. She whirled round, her arms automatically crossing protectively over her breasts. He was standing just inside the doorway, naked save for a pair of white cotton boxers which did little to conceal the state of his arousal.

The pupils of his eyes were so dilated they had covered the iris and there was a tension about the way he held himself which told her that he had been there, watching her, for quite some time. She took a step back as he moved towards her, his whole demeanour predatory.

'*Non,*' he said, huskily. 'Do not conceal yourself from me.'

He reached for her and enclosed her wrists, gently but insistently pulling them away from her body. Anna's heart hammered erratically in her chest as his eyes raked over her nakedness, and she shivered involuntarily as they rested on the agitated rise and fall of her breasts.

She knew she should cover herself, order him out of her bedroom, yet somehow she could not force the words through her lips. A part of her, the yearning, needy part that she had been forced to hide for so long, cried out to her to be still, not to be afraid, and she listened to its voice.

'*Mon Dieu*, Anna, how exquisite you are!'

Dominic placed the tips of his first and second fingers against the pulse which beat wildly at the base of her throat and rested them there for a moment before lightly running them down, between her breasts to her navel. Then he turned her, gently, so that she was once again facing the mirror.

Anna could not take her eyes from his smooth, brown hands as they rested at her waist, the long, elegant fingers touching over her softly rounded stomach. Slowly, he moved them upwards, running his fingertips along the undersides of her heavy breasts and cupping them in his palms as she had done only moments before. As he lifted them, their pale pink-tipped crowns hardened to lightly puckered roses, the nipples like two smooth buttons.

She leaned against him as he passed his fingers over them, circling the areolae with his fingertips until they tautened to the point of discomfort.

'That is good, no?' he whispered, his breath hot in her ear. 'You see?'

He ran his fingertips over her upper chest where a faint pink blush was spreading under her skin. Dominic picked up a hank of her hair and smoothed it over her shoulder, over one breast. Then he repeated the action with the other side so that she looked like a latter day Lady Godiva, her glossy gold-blonde tresses covering her to her waist.

Dominic stroked his hands over the heavy silk of her hair and began to wind each side around his fingers, into two smooth ropes. As the hair was gathered up, her pink nipples peeked through until they were naked again and Dominic had the two ropes in his hands.

Anna held her breath as he crossed each side over the other at her chest, so that his left hand held the rope of hair from her right side and vice versa. Then he slowly wound each skein around the opposite breast, lifting and separating them.

He tightened the makeshift halter he had fashioned from her hair around her body, almost to the point of discomfort. Their eyes met in the mirror and Anna let out her pent up breath on a sigh as she saw the enigmatic expression in his. She did not understand it, but she felt she recognised the way he was looking at her. Knew, at least, that it was the cause of the heavy, sexual warmth which was now spreading rapidly through her body.

Dominic smiled slowly at her and, pressing a kiss against the side of her neck, he let the hair go, watching it as it unravelled and fell in soft waves about her breasts.

Anna swallowed as his hands smoothed down her sides, squeezed her buttocks briefly, then swept round to her trembling thighs. The back of his hand brushed against the golden fleece at their apex.

'So soft. Such a rare and lovely colour. And inside. . .'

Mesmerised by the soft, husky cadence of his voice, Anna forgot to protest as he gently parted her thighs and exposed the pale pink jewel between them. The tender folds of flesh had swelled, glistening with moisture as he opened them.

'Oh!' Anna gasped at the first, light touch of his fingers against her sex, her legs almost giving way beneath her. Dominic turned her in his arms and she shuddered convulsively.

His lips were unexpectedly cool as he moved them across her face, kissing her temples, her eyelids, the curve of her jaw to the base of her ear. He murmured something in French as he pressed a kiss against the corner of her mouth, then the tip of his hot tongue traced a line along her mouth so that it opened like a flower in the sun and invited him in.

Anna clung to his shoulders as he kissed her, her head spinning dizzily and her eyes fluttering to a close. The coarse hairs on his bare chest rasped against her tender skin as her breasts were flattened against him. She could feel his erection pressing urgently against the soft swell of her stomach, his hands roaming freely across her back and down to her bottom.

All rational thought had fled, nothing mattered now but the easing of the ache which was building between her thighs. Anna welcomed the heated invasion of his tongue into her mouth. She drew it in, circling it with her own, her fingernails digging into the velvety skin of his shoulders as she sought to keep her balance.

Suddenly, without breaking the kiss, he swept

her up into his arms. Drawing away from her slightly, his eyes burned into hers. She was boneless, liquid, totally in his control. Her arms snaked around his neck and she leaned her head against the hard cushion of his shoulder. A few short strides took them to the bed and he laid her down on it before straightening.

His eyes never left her face as he quickly dispensed with his boxer shorts. Anna's eyes skittered down to where his cock reared up between his thighs. It was long and thick, the dark pink, circumcised tip smooth, a teardrop of moisture glistening at its end.

Anna reached for it as he lay down beside her on the rumpled sheets. It was hot to the touch and so hard, so demanding, that for a moment Anna felt afraid. She ran her hand along the silky shaft, tentatively at first, afraid that, like Paul, he would rebuff her. But Dominic simply lay and watched her, his eyes hooded, his body held taut, in suspension.

His cock twitched slightly under her hand as she stroked it and she ran her palm upward, across the taut plane of his stomach to his chest. The hair which curled across his pectorals and arrowed down to his groin was thick and black, coarse, yet surprisingly silky to the touch. Anna tangled her fingers in it, brushing the tips against one nipple. It hardened and, fascinated, she repeated the exercise with the other one.

Suddenly, Dominic leaned forward and kissed her, lightly, on the lips, before dipping his head to take one of her nipples into his hot mouth. Anna lay back and stared up at the ceiling, seeing nothing as he suckled first one, then the other. The pull of his mouth at her breast created an answering tug deep in her womb.

When his questing fingers touched again against the hard bud which nestled in the slippery folds of her vulva, Anna gasped, suddenly afraid. She reached down to cover his hand with her own.

'Anna?' he whispered, gently bringing her hand up and placing it against his heart.

She could feel it throbbing steadily against her palm and, inexplicably, some of her fear receded. Dominic scanned her eyes, frowning as if puzzled, then he smiled.

'It's all right, *chérie* – hold on to me. Close your eyes. Trust me.'

Reassured, she allowed her eyelids to droop and, bringing both arms up around his neck, she tightened her grip. This time when his sensitive fingers invaded the secret garden of her sex, she sighed and melted against him.

Warmth radiated out from between her thighs as he unerringly found that small, erotic centre and began to caress it, his movements rhythmic, in time with the throb of his heart against her chest. He played her like a delicate musical instrument, reverently, yet with a sureness of touch which made her dig her nails into his flesh. She could feel herself opening to him, inviting his questing fingers in.

His warm breath caressed her ear as he whispered to her, half in French, yet it did not matter that she didn't understand the words, for it was his tone, the rhythm of his speech which moved her.

'So beautiful. . .'

29

The warmth was building to a crescendo now, invading her limbs and spiralling up, along her spine, and for a split second Anna was terrified, opening her eyes wide in anguish. Dominic kissed her, hard, sucking out her fear until at last she was wracked by spasm after spasm of joyful release.

Pulling her mouth away from his, she threw back her head and cried out, sure she could not bear the intensity of it. Dominic held his hand tightly against her pulsating core, prolonging the sensation until she begged him to let her go.

She cried out again, this time in anguish as he took his hand away, but he did not abandon her for long, entering her quickly, before her orgasm had completely ebbed away.

Anna wrapped herself around him, tears of joy, love, gratitude; she did not know what emotion, streaming down her face as she was filled by him. She could feel him moving inside her and she met him, thrust for thrust, grinding her hips against his as he raced towards his own climax.

Her cries of ecstasy mingled with his as they rolled together, still enmeshed, on the bed. And the one thought that played over and over through Anna's mind was that this was it, the thing that she had always suspected she had been missing. And she knew that never again would she be content to settle for anything less.

As they peeled apart, Dominic gathered her into the safe, warm circle of his arms and cradled her against his sweat-slicked body. The glitter of his eyes caressed her in the darkness as he smoothed the flat of his hand across her flanks and up her back, to the top of her spine. Massaging the base of her skull, he kissed her with a lingering hunger.

'I never knew . . . I never guessed,' she blurted suddenly.

Dominic raised himself up on one elbow and traced the line of her jaw thoughtfully with his forefinger. Then he gripped her chin firmly between finger and thumb and bent back her head so that he could stare deep into her eyes.

'There is more, *ma petite* . . . so much more than that.'

He did not smile, merely stared at her intently, waiting for his words to register. Anna was mesmerised by the expression in his eyes and somewhere, deep within her, something stirred.

'I want you to teach me,' she whispered hoarsely.

He smiled.

'*Mais oui*, Anna – I intend to.'

Chapter Three

... *SHE WAS STANDING* in the middle of a field of rapeseed. Its pungent odour was heavy on the warm air and it clogged her throat. All around her, as far as the eye could see, was a yellow ocean, rippling in never-ending waves as the summer breeze passed over it and lifted her heavy, unrestrained hair. A heat haze hovered so that everything around her shimmered, adding to the sense of unreality.

She was naked. There was a peculiar tension in the air, a sort of breathless, erotic anticipation. She heard a rustle behind her and smiled. Turning slowly, she saw him standing quite still, watching her.

He did not speak. His face was intent as he walked towards her. She knew that this was what she had been waiting for and she held out her arms to him. He caught hold of her hands and pulled them up, around his neck, so that her naked body was flattened against the harsh denim and slippery silk of his jeans and shirt. The fabric chafed her tender skin and she sighed, throwing back her head boldly, exposing her throat to his lips.

His lips were cool against her skin before he raised his head and caught her gaze with his. His eyes smouldered down at her as he passed them over her face, finally coming to rest on her parted lips. She clung to him as he lowered her gently to the ground and she felt the soft, moist earth, cool beneath her. As her body brushed against the rapeseed flowers, a puff of yellow powder rose up in a cloud around them, patterning her skin.

She held her breath as he slowly lowered his head, her eyes closing in anticipation of the delicious pressure of his mouth on hers . . .

Anna woke with a start, just before their lips fused. Reaching out for Dominic, she encountered an empty pillow and she groaned. Sitting bolt upright in bed, she clasped the duvet tightly around her heated body. It took a few minutes to come to, for her racing heartbeat to slow and her shallow breathing to normalise.

The dream had seemed so real, was so vivid, she could feel the moisture of arousal gathering between her thighs. She smiled slowly as she recalled the events of the night before.

Anna squeezed her legs together tightly and hugged her knees to her. It didn't matter that he hadn't been here when she awoke, he had promised there would be more.

Her reflection in the bathroom mirror when she dragged herself to it spoke all too clearly of the disturbed night she had spent. Apart from the initial satiated sleep she had fallen into after she and Dominic had made love, her night had been restless, punctuated by fragmented, erotic dreams such as the one in the field of rapeseed which left her feeling dissatisfied and unfulfilled.

Anna spent longer than usual in the bathroom, emerging into the bedroom at last with full make-up intact. Telling herself that she wasn't taking any more care with her appearance than she did on any other morning, she nevertheless pulled her newest satin bra and brief set from her drawer.

The pale apricot colour glowed prettily against her skin, lending it some of the material's lustre. The matching suspender belt she had bought in a sudden fit of longing had never actually been worn and she pulled it out of the drawer now, fingering the stiff fabric uncertainly.

She wasn't used to the sense of restraint, the tightness of the band around her waist, yet she found it curiously comfortable. It fitted neatly at the lowest part of her waist where her hips flared gently outward. The fine, skin-coloured nylon stockings which she took from the unopened pack whispered against her skin as she eased them up her legs.

Anna took a moment to admire the effect in the mirror. The naked skin at the tops of her thighs looked very white, the frame provided by the taut suspenders drawing the eye to her satin-covered pubis. Running her eyes up her midline, she noted with satisfaction the way in which the apricot satin moulded her heavy breasts into two perfect globes, the creamy skin spilling over the top, creating a cleavage to be proud of.

None of her working clothes were very alluring, so she opted for her comfortable, caramel-coloured suit. As she fastened the zip on the short, straight skirt over one hip, Anna was aware of her every movement, as if her skin had become sensitised.

In a mood of uncharacteristic self-indulgence, she slipped into her one silk blouse, noticing as she did so how its rich, clotted cream colour toned with her skirt. She was almost reluctant to cover it up with the unstructured jacket, so she took it downstairs over her arm, leaving it on the hall chair with her handbag.

Just as she was wriggling her feet into her shoes, Anna sensed she was not alone in the hallway. She turned slowly, preparing herself for the usual jolt she felt on seeing Dominic. It was no use; her stomach still plummeted as her eyes drank him in greedily. She blushed as she recalled the way he had looked at her in the field of her dreams.

This morning he was wearing a crisp cotton, sky blue shirt, the short sleeves of which exposed his tightly muscled forearms. Anna's eyes lingered on the black hairs sprinkled generously over the bronzed skin, remembering how their silky coarseness had felt to the touch. Her fingers itched to reach out and stroke them.

'Good morning, Anna.'

Her eyes flew up and met the enigmatic expression in his. She had the sudden, uncomfortable feeling that he could read her thoughts, that he knew her every desire. Her mouth felt suddenly, inexplicably dry as he moved towards her, slowly, like a predatory animal about to pounce.

'Dominic . . .'

His name barely whispered across her lips as his mouth covered hers in a brief, hard kiss which left her breathless. He smiled as he pulled away, a small, knowing smile which made excitement curl in her stomach. It plummeted again in disappointment as he turned on his heel and preceded her into the kitchen.

Anna was so affected by the small exchange that she toyed with her toast and coffee, her appetite gone. Dominic, however, had no such inhibitions and she watched him eat, single-minded even in this.

After breakfast, Anna drove him to the University and took him into Alan's inner sanctum. They parted company then, with Anna taking her place at her work station and Dominic and Alan going straight to the lecture theatre where Dominic was scheduled to speak later that morning.

It was a long morning. Routine tasks which Anna normally performed without thinking were suddenly irritating to her. She imagined Dominic preparing to speak to the Business Studies students and envied them, wishing she could be there.

As if she had spoken aloud, Alan came across and asked if she would like to accompany him to the lecture theatre.

'You might find it interesting, Anna, especially since you now know Dominic. He's a born communicator.'

You don't have to tell me that! she thought wryly. But, much as she wanted to go, she was snowed under with typing.

'I haven't finished these . . .'

Anna was relieved when Alan waved a dismissive hand at her dutiful, if half-hearted, protest and she grabbed her bag eagerly, before he had the chance to change his mind.

The lecture theatre was a large, Victorian auditorium with staggered seats. Because she was with Alan, Anna was seated in the front row, but discreetly to one side. Dominic spotted her the moment he walked on to the stage and his smile sent shivers of pleasurable warmth right through her.

He was an inspirational speaker; his deep, mellifluous voice with its sexy French accent resonated around the hall, affecting most of the females present, Anna decided, taking a crafty look around her. His obvious love for his subject shone through his words. Passing on his knowledge, his boundless enthusiasm, was quite obviously a joy to him.

Anna listened, spellbound, to the sound of his voice. As the lecture continued, she found herself caught up in it, enthralled by the speaker as much as by his words. He used his hands extensively to illustrate each point. Anna could not tear her eyes away from his long, sensitive fingers, the memory of them moving over her skin, drawing a response from her and making her feel hot, removed from the others in the hall.

At last, the auditorium erupted into applause and he threw the subject open for discussion.

Questions flew thick and fast, evidence of the interest he had generated during the past hour. He answered every one thoughtfully, courteous to each and every student so that, when they were finally satisfied, he looked exhausted. At last, reluctantly, they let him go.

'Bravo, Dominic!' Alan climbed on to the stage and clapped him on the shoulder as the last of the students filed out and there were just the three of them left. 'Thank you so much – and that is just the beginning, eh? How about a spot of lunch?'

Dominic's eyes sought Anna's and she smiled, suddenly feeling ridiculously shy.

'Will Anna be joining us?'

Alan looked momentarily surprised. Recovering himself, he beamed as if he thought it an excellent idea.

'Certainly – you will join us, won't you, Anna?'

'Well, I . . . ' Anna wasn't sure whether Alan wanted her to refuse. It wasn't usual for him to take her to lunch with the visiting lecturers, even when she was acting as their temporary landlady.

Dominic came to her rescue. 'That is settled, then. A moment, please, while I . . . uh . . . freshen up.'

Seeing that Alan was not at all put out by her accompanying them, Anna paid a swift visit to the Ladies' to re-touch her make-up.

Alan took them to a small, quiet bistro, just as Anna had guessed he would. The head waiter greeted him by name, and they were seated with great ceremony at a round corner table by the window. The table was small enough for Anna to be able to feel the presence of both men either side of her, Dominic to her left, Alan to her right. But while Alan politely kept to his own space, Dominic's lower leg pressed close to hers.

They ordered; tender chicken breasts poached in white wine and bathed in cream, soft ribbons of pasta in a spicy mushroom sauce. Alan tucked in with relish. Anna, feeling Dominic's dark eyes on her as she ate, picked at her food self-consciously.

Dominic's leg against hers was warm and insistent. Dabbing at her lips with a napkin, she met his eyes boldly. The tension fairly crackled between them, so that Anna wondered if Alan had noticed it. But no, he was endearingly oblivious.

Anna did not know how he was managing it, but Dominic was carrying on a perfectly normal if desultory conversation with Alan whilst making love to her with his eyes. Their feet entwined, leather against leather, under the table. Anna sipped constantly at her wine, trying in vain to counteract the dryness of her mouth and throat.

As they finished the first course, Dominic tipped back his wine glass and drained the contents with one swallow. Anna could not take her eyes from his smooth, golden-skinned throat as his Adam's apple moved along its length. His neck was strong, barely lined. Anna guessed he was probably thirty-three or four, at least ten years her senior. Experienced.

She started as she suddenly realised that the conversation had stopped and both men were looking at her expectantly. There was a definite gleam of amusement in Dominic's eyes.

'Er . . . sorry?'

Alan shot her a puzzled frown and she realised that she must pull herself together somehow, at least during working hours.

'I only asked you what you wanted for pudding, Anna?' Alan repeated.

'Oh, I see. Sorry. Could I see the menu, please?'

Anna's eyes barely took in the printed words, so she ordered the first thing on the list. Strawberries and cream.

Again, she was conscious of Dominic's steady regard while she ate. The soft fruit and thick, cool cream caressed her throat as they slipped down and she swallowed hard, sure Dominic could read her every thought.

When they had all finished, Alan excused himself and made for the Gents'. As soon as he disappeared, Dominic leaned towards her, napkin in hand, and gently dabbed at the corner of her mouth.

'Cream,' he whispered, his eyes burning into hers as he came closer.

Anna ran the tip of her tongue nervously along her lips. Dominic's eyes narrowed as they followed the motion, then dipped lower, to her breasts. Anna blushed as she realised that the outline of her hardening nipples must be clearly visible through her bra and the thin silk of her blouse.

Squirming slightly in her seat, Anna felt sure that Dominic was aware of her state of arousal. She gasped as he suddenly leaned across the table and pressed the pad of his thumb against one burgeoning nipple.

Glancing nervously from left to right, Anna

resisted the instinctive urge to pull away. Dominic smiled slowly, the expression in his eyes sending a tremor of feeling through her that was uncomfortably close to fear.

Then he withdrew his hand and Anna saw that Alan was wending his way back to their table. She felt hot and trembly as he sat down, nodding feebly when he asked her if she would like coffee.

She stiffened as, suddenly, she felt Dominic's hand on her thigh. Glancing nervously at Alan, she saw that he was concentrating on lighting up his pipe. The coffee arrived with cheese and biscuits and both men helped themselves. Anna cut herself a portion of Brie and took two wafer-thin crackers from the plate.

As the soft, creamy cheese touched her tongue, Dominic's hand inched further up her leg, concealed by the voluminous table cloth. Anna stared straight ahead as his fingers reached the soft skin above her stockings and he began to trace little circles, round and round, with his fingertips.

Anna glanced around her, close to panic as he began to stroke her through the thin satin of her panties. Leaning back in his chair, Alan had the air of a man who was content with the world. Dominic concentrated on his coffee and cheese. To their left, a young couple stared into each other's eyes over lasagne and salad, while to their right a large table of dark-suited men discussed business and sport. None appeared to have any inkling of what was happening under the tablecloth at their table.

Unable to help herself, Anna slackened her

thighs, allowing them to fall apart so that he had access to her warm sex. Insinuating his fingers under the tight elastic of her briefs, Dominic stroked along her moist crevices, brushing teasingly across the hard bud which yearned for his touch.

Anna had to stop eating, concentrating desperately on keeping her breathing under control. Arranging her face into a socially acceptable expression, she bore down on his probing fingers, rubbing herself against them as the heat between her legs grew.

God, if anybody knew, if anybody realised! A hot wave of shame washed over her as her hips jerked and she came, biting hard on her lower lip to stop herself from crying out.

She gripped the table as Dominic withdrew his hand. A waiter approached the table.

'How was the meal?' he asked politely as he replenished the coffee cups.

Anna merely smiled inanely, trying to get rid of the glazed look she knew was in her eyes.

'Excellent,' Dominic answered, bringing the fingers which he had just withdrawn from her body to his lips and kissing them theatrically.

He turned then and caught Anna's eye. She could not read his expression, but it frightened her. Muttering her excuses, she fled to the Ladies'.

Once in the sanctuary of the ladies' cloakroom, Anna leaned her heated forehead against the cold glass of the full-length mirror which was screwed to the wall. Her cheeks were flushed, her eyes unnaturally bright, so much so that she was surprised Alan had failed to notice.

As she stepped back from the mirror, she saw that her blouse was still stretched taut over her breasts, the dark pink shadow of her nipples easily discernible. Holding her wrists under the cold tap, she concentrated on breathing deeply and evenly, determined to regain her equilibrium before returning to the table.

Marginally calmer, Anna emerged from the Ladies'. And found Dominic waiting for her.

'Dominic. . .!'

Without a word, he took her by the hand and pulled her through a door marked *Private – Staff Only*. They were in a cupboard, full to brimming with cleaning equipment and stores. Anna recognised the sticky, cloying scent of lavender wax as Dominic closed the door behind them and pushed her up against it.

'Dominic!' she whispered urgently. 'Not here! Oh God!'

He had pushed up her short, tight skirt and was already dragging down her apricot satin briefs. Anna's legs went weak as his probing fingers closed over her hot, wet sex. She caught the glint of his smile in the darkness as he encountered the well of her arousal and entered her with two fingers while, with the other hand, he unfastened his trousers.

Bending her leg at the knee, he lifted it up, over his hip, lifting her with two hands about her waist as he thrust into her without preamble. Supporting her weight against the door, he buried his face in her hair which was escaping from its neat roll and falling in abandon around her shoulders. Her legs were stretched wide apart, one foot balancing precariously on the floor by the toes.

The increasing rhythm of his breathing against her ear inflamed Anna further and she clutched at his shoulders, pressing her pelvis forward so that her swollen clitoris was rubbing against the hair-roughened skin of his lower belly.

She sensed the moment when he reached the point of no return and bore down, releasing the pent up pressure in the core of her. They came together, Anna with a small, anguished cry, Dominic with a stream of words in his own tongue which curled around her, intensifying her pleasure.

He collapsed against her, winding her, and she moaned softly. She would never have believed that such a short interlude of hot, sweaty sex could make her feel so good. Dominic's lips brushed almost tenderly across her forehead.

Struggling to pull up her briefs and roll her tailored skirt back over her thighs, Anna froze as a knock sounded on the door outside.

'What's going on in there? 'Ello? Is there someone in there?'

Anna stood stock-still, willing the man to go away. Her heart hammered wildly in her chest, the blood pounding in her ears at the mere thought of being discovered.

Dominic, though, barely paused in buttoning his fly, taking her by surprise as he grabbed her hand. As soon as her weight was away from the door, he opened it.

'Sorry to keep you,' he said with unbelievable nonchalance as the young waiter regarded them with astonishment. 'Some things, they will not wait, you know?'

Anna's face burned scarlet as he pulled her after him along the corridor. She could feel the young man's eyes boring into her back and she was unable to resist the urge to look over her shoulder at him. Incredulity was written all over his face, mixed with a kind of awed envy and Anna quickly averted her eyes.

She stopped at the entrance to the restaurant and did what she could to fix her hair. Her skirt was rumpled beyond redemption, but she ran her hands over it ineffectually anyway.

'What will you do about this?' Dominic asked her, amused as he passed a fingertip softly over her swollen mouth. 'Or these – they shine too brightly.'

Anna blinked as he kissed the corners of her eyes.

'Alan won't notice,' she whispered, a trifle desperately. 'Oh, Dominic, how could you? I am so embarrassed!'

But the reproach did not sound nearly as aggrieved as she had intended and he laughed at her, so richly that she could not summon up any indignation.

'Where have you two been?' Alan grumbled mildly as they approached the table.

Anna imagined that his eyes passed briefly over her flushed face and dishevelled hair and she blushed furiously.

'Ah well, um, never mind. I've, er, I've settled the bill. We should be getting back now.'

The waiter who had found them in the broom cupboard opened the door for them. As Anna passed and caught his eye, he winked and she almost fell down the steps in her hurry to get out. Dominic's hand came to steady her by the elbow and she could tell by the way he squeezed it that he had seen the exchange and was somehow pleased by it.

'I've arranged a tutorial for this afternoon, Dominic,' Alan was saying as they waited for a taxi, 'and I'm afraid the Chamber of Commerce meeting I was telling you about will keep us all evening, and half the night too, I shouldn't wonder. So I've left tomorrow free. The weather forecast is excellent, I thought you might like to get out into the countryside.'

'Perfect,' Dominic opened the door of the black cab which drew up.

Alan climbed in first, followed by Anna. It was the kind of high step up which made it impossible to get in and out elegantly. Dominic caressed her raised bottom as she climbed in and Anna landed on the seat beside Alan, blushing scarlet. She did not dare to look at Dominic as he slipped in beside her.

'It would be nice to get out in the fresh air for a while,' he said conversationally as they drew away. 'Perhaps, Alan, you would do me the favour of lending me your beautiful secretary for the day?'

Alan looked surprised.

'Well, of course, Dominic, if Anna is happy. . .?'

Anna smiled awkwardly.

'If you're sure, Alan,' she said with as much nonchalance as she could muster.

'Good. Perhaps we could take a picnic, Anna?'

She turned and caught Dominic's eye. Her heart fluttered in her chest and she saw that the lightness of his smile was contradicted by the intensity in his eyes.

'A picnic?' she murmured weakly. 'That would be lovely.'

Chapter Four

DOMINIC DID NOT return home with Anna
when she finished work that evening. Instead,
Alan kept him back to discuss the schedule for the
week, warning Anna that he would take him on
afterwards to the Chamber of Commerce meeting.

Behind his back, Dominic made a face at Anna,
his eyes leaving her in no doubt where he would
rather be – in bed, with her.

'Take my spare door-key,' she told him,
rummaging for it in the bottom of her shoulder
bag. 'That way you won't feel awkward about
coming home late . . .'

She trailed off as she realised she had used the
word *home*, wondering for the first time what his
own home was like, whether he had someone
waiting for him there. Seeing the uncertainty
chase across her features, Dominic frowned
slightly, closing his hand over hers as he took the
key from her and giving it a squeeze.

Anna had just drifted into sleep when she
heard Dominic turn the key she had lent him in

the lock. Every nerve ending tingled as she listened to his footsteps on the stairs, coming closer. They paused on the landing and Anna held her breath, half willing him to turn her way, the other half of her hoping he'd go to his own room. Anna exhaled slowly as his footsteps continued away from her.

It frightened her, this excess of passion he had awoken in her and, if she was truthful, she had to admit that she was a little afraid of Dominic himself. There was something about the way he looked at her, sometimes, that made her feel she was a mere puppet dancing to his whim. And that what was to him a mere dalliance could easily become very important to her.

And then there was the fact that when she was with him . . . like that . . . she barely knew herself. He only had to touch her in a certain way, speak to her in a certain tone of voice, and she found herself doing things that she would never contemplate in her more rational moments.

Like the incident in the restaurant. Her cheeks grew hot even now as she thought about it. First the casual giving of pleasure beneath the tablecloth, then the quick, savage coupling in a broom cupboard . . . Anna trembled with the remembered shame which, somehow, was interspersed with the most exquisite pleasure.

Closing her eyes against the memory, she tried to sleep.

It was later when Anna was woken by the soft swish of the door opening and closing. She yawned and stretched, still soft with sleep, before opening her eyes to find Dominic's shadowy figure looming over her bed. He was naked save for a pair of boxer shorts and Anna could smell the clean, masculine heat of him as he leaned over her. He reached out and touched her shoulder as she instinctively sat up, pushing her back on to the bed.

Anna felt the blood stir in her veins as his eyes glittered down at her in the darkness and he pulled back the duvet. She shivered as the air touched her bare skin where it was exposed by the thin-strapped nightdress. Circling one of her wrists easily in his hand, Dominic brought it up, above her head. With the other hand, he brought the other one up to join it, so that her arms were both stretched above her head, her wrists held in one of his hands.

She felt vulnerable but, although she supposed she could easily pull free if she wished, she lay acquiescent before him. She could not suppress a gasp as he suddenly ripped her nightdress away from her body with his free hand, flinging the ruined garment to one side.

'Dominic . . .!'

'Quiet!'

Anna's words dried on her tongue as his grip tightened on her wrists and his eyes flashed dangerously at her. Excitement, threaded through with an exquisite edge of fear, kept her immobile, waiting to see what he would do next. Her body was no longer limp and relaxed, but taut, bristling with anticipation.

As her eyes gradually accustomed themselves to the darkness, Anna saw Dominic's lips curve into a smile. She shivered as he ran his forefinger from the frantically beating pulse at the base of her throat down, between her breasts, circling her navel and coming to rest deep within the soft hair of her mound where it sought the small, sleeping button of her desire.

As soon as he found it, he applied enough pressure to awaken it and Anna closed her eyes as the familiar, welcome warmth invaded her limbs. Without taking his finger off the point of pressure, Dominic moved the swelling nub round and round until the juices began to flow, seeping out of her.

'Open your eyes.'

His voice was low, but authoritative, and Anna obeyed him instantly. He ran his eyes along the length of her naked body and Anna followed his gaze. Her nipples had swollen to two pink, turgid peaks and beyond them, her legs had parted slightly in response to the light pressure between her thighs.

Her entire body seemed to quiver, taut as a bow string as he slowly lowered his head and took one puckered nipple into his mouth. As he suckled her, Anna could feel an answering pull in her womb which in turn transmitted itself to her straining clitoris.

Slowly, Anna was taken over by sensation to the exclusion of all rational thought. Somewhere in the back of her mind she urged herself to resist, to stay in control this time, but her body would not listen. So that when Dominic straightened and released her hands, she made no move to bring them down to her sides, and her thighs clutched convulsively at his fingers as he withdrew them from her needy sex.

Dominic ignored her whispered protest.

'Open your legs,' he commanded.

Anna obliged, sliding her heels over the smooth slipperiness of the cool cotton sheet.

'Raise your knees – open wider. I want to look at you.'

Anna closed her eyes momentarily on the shame of displaying herself thus. She swallowed at her dry throat as he moved to the end of the bed and feasted his eyes on her.

'Ah, *chérie* – how wet you are! How ready.'

Anna could have wept with shame. A small, anguished cry caught in her throat. Dominic smiled and moved round the bed to kiss her on the lips. The kiss was unexpectedly tender, his lips moving over hers in a featherlight caress. Anna felt a sudden, overwhelming need to be filled by him, to welcome him into her body and wrap her legs around him, binding him to her.

'What is it you want, Anna?'

She blushed as he whispered the words against her mouth.

'Tell me, *chérie*.'

'I . . . I . . .'

The words stuck in her throat and she squirmed slightly, hoping that he would not make her say them. But he was not in a mood to let her off lightly.

'Yes, Anna? Say the words – I want to hear them on your lips.'

'I want you to make love to me,' she said on a rush, running the words into each other.

Dominic flicked his eyes along the length of her

body, as if considering. Almost carelessly, he played with the damp curls which shielded her glistening sex until she writhed helplessly beneath his hand, desperate for release.

'Please . . .!' she whispered.

He smiled, a cool, hard smile and she knew at once what he wanted to hear her say. Sheer desperation made her bold.

'Fuck me, Dominic! Please, please, just fuck me. Now!'

She held out her arms to him and gathered him to her as his strong, lean body covered hers. Slowly, so slowly Anna felt she would weep with impatience, he inched his hard cock into her welcoming body.

A fine sweat broke out all over her as he thrust with iron control, his strokes long and leisurely. Holding him to her with her heels at the small of his back, Anna tried to prevent him from withdrawing.

'Please . . . ' she moaned as the pressure built, 'harder . . . oh . . . oh God! Yes!'

At last he quickened his pace, sinking into her more deeply with each pumping thrust until they were both consumed with heat. They rolled together on the bed in a tangle of limbs. Anna dug her nails into his shoulders as he plundered her mouth with his tongue, holding her almost painfully by the hair.

They climaxed together on a rush of heat, their bodies melded together as one, tears of joy and disbelief spilling on to Anna's cheeks. Dominic made no attempt to withdraw from her, merely rolling them on to their side so that they were facing each other, still entwined as they fell asleep.

Once again, when Anna awoke she was alone. Her sweat-soaked hair had dried on her forehead, the remains of their shared fluids staining her inner thighs. Memories of her wild abandonment of the night before crowded into her mind, sending the heat rushing into her cheeks. How was she going to face him? Groaning slightly, Anna hauled herself off to the bathroom.

Showering away the reminders of the night before, she washed her hair, feeling human again. Opening the bedroom curtains, she blinked at the bright sunlight streaming through the open window. The air was fresh with the promise of another warm, sunny day and she breathed it in deeply. It was a perfect day for a picnic.

After battling with the tangles in her hair, she left it to dry naturally while she dressed. It fell in damp fronds about her face as she stepped into a bright floral sun dress which buttoned up the front.

Underneath she wore a front fastening, strapless bra and plain white cotton briefs, more practical than sexy. Lacing canvas deck shoes on her feet, she decided to leave her hair loose, clipping it off her face at the sides with two large yellow clips which matched the sunflowers on her dress.

Running down the stairs, she was surprised to smell coffee.

'Dominic! You're up early!'

Turning towards her he raised an eyebrow in gentle irony. 'It's ten o'clock – you overslept, no?'

'Ten o'clock!' Anna repeated, aghast. She hadn't bothered to check the clock, assuming she had woken at her normal time. 'You should have woken me.'

He shrugged.

'I didn't have the heart. Sit down – this is ready.'

Anna obeyed, bemused by him.

'Where did you get all this?'

'I've been out to shop for our picnic. And all you had for breakfast was cereals and bread,' he admonished with a laugh, dunking a croissant in his coffee. 'Mon Dieu, Anna – how do you live?'

She smiled and tucked into her breakfast. The butter melted sinfully on to the hot pastry as she smeared it with strawberry jam.

'That was lovely,' she said, pushing her empty plate away. 'Thank you.'

Taking her by the hand, Dominic picked up the enormous basket he had packed and pulled her out of the kitchen. He moved the basket away from her prying eyes as they walked through the hall.

'Whatever have you got in there?'

'Wait and see,' he told her.

Anna wound back the sun-roof on her Peugeot and the sun streamed through on to their heads. Dominic was wearing a red piqué polo shirt and tight denim jeans which moulded the outline of his tautly muscled thighs. He looked relaxed as they drove out of town, the wind through the sun-roof ruffling his hair out of its usual neatness, the sun warming his tanned skin so that it glowed gold.

Heading for the Downs, Anna wondered what could be in the basket. Slanting a sideways glance at Dominic, she wondered if he would make love to her on the Downs? No, there would be too many people about, she would have to wait until this evening.

It being a weekday, though, there weren't many cars in the official car park. They began to walk at a leisurely pace, following one of the designated pathways. Taking her by the hand, as if it were the most natural thing in the world, Dominic steered her off the main pathway.

'Come – let us find a quiet spot where we can watch the world go by until we are ready to eat.'

Anna nodded and they walked hand in hand off the path, through a small copse of trees. Once through it they found an area far hillier than the plain across which they had just walked and it was easy to find a private place.

Dominic took a blanket from out of the basket and spread it on the ground.

'You've thought of everything!' Anna smiled as she sat down on it.

'All the important things,' he agreed, uncorking a bottle of champagne.

Anna laughed as the golden liquid fizzed and overflowed. Dominic had even brought two long, slender-stemmed glasses and he handed her one now. The champagne was crisp and tart on her tongue, the bubbles rising to tickle her nose. Once her glass was empty, she put it aside and lay back on the blanket.

The sun was warm on her face and her bare arms and legs. She could hear a cricket close by, louder than the distant drone of traffic. The grass smelt fresh and moist as it swayed in the light breeze. Anna felt drowsy, content and she closed her eyes with a sigh.

Dominic raised himself up on one elbow and trailed a ticklish path around her jawline with a frond of wild grass.

'How long have you been married, Anna?' he asked unexpectedly.

Anna opened one eye. 'Why do you ask?'

Dominic shrugged and grimaced. 'That first time – that was your first *petit mort, n'est-ce pas*?'

She nodded warily.

'And how long have you been married?'

It was a fair enough question in the circumstances, but Anna knew that it was irrelevant. 'Five years,' she replied.

'Five years?'

'Yes. Paul says I am frigid.'

Dominic's stupefied expression was so comical that she laughed.

'And you, Anna – is that what you thought too?'

She flushed. 'Sometimes I thought . . . no, not really. I nearly believed him though. You came along just in time!'

'This I do not understand.'

Dominic shook his head as if in wonder at the idea. He seemed genuinely curious about her lack of sexual experience and, to her surprise, his questions did not offend her. They were, after all, questions she had often asked herself. And at that moment, Anna loved him for his incredulity.

'How could you be married for five years and

yet never experience an orgasm with your husband?'

'I don't know . . . he . . . he has never touched me as you did. He just . . . gets on with it, I suppose. Then he rolls over and goes to sleep.'

'Mon Dieu! The man deserves to be shot! Yet I do not understand – how can this be?'

He looked so perplexed that Anna felt a spark of mischief.

'I'll show you. Here,' she arranged herself on her back, knees bent as if for a gynaecological examination. 'Now, imagine that you are Paul. Lie on top of me, between my legs – that's right. Make a bridge with your arms either side of me, careful not to touch! Now, wriggle your hips, thrust in and out for exactly four and a half minutes. I know that's right, because I timed him once, by the digital bedside clock. No, don't look at me! You must stare at the interesting pattern on the iron bedhead . . . Dominic!'

He collapsed to one side of her, laughing uncontrollably and Anna sat up, rearranging the skirt of her sundress primly around her knees.

'You are joking, no?' he choked.

'No, unfortunately I am not.'

'This is unbelievable. It is criminal!'

Their shared laughter was cleansing, helping to heal the hurt of the past five, arid years. Suddenly, Dominic stopped laughing and slowly lowered his head. The touch of his lips on hers made her feel like liquid beneath him. She welcomed the demanding press of his body against hers as the kiss deepened and became exploring.

'Are you hungry?' he murmured as he broke away.

She shook her head and he smiled, pulling the basket towards them. Anna watched through half closed eyes as he brought out a punnet of ready hulled strawberries and a little glass jug full of thick double cream. Dipping one, small strawberry into it, he pressed it between her teeth.

As Anna swallowed, Dominic kissed her, licking the sweet juice of the fruit from her lips. Her arms curled up, around his neck and she arched against him. His fingertips traced small circles lightly against the bare skin of her throat, working his way across her chest to the first button of her dress.

Briefly, it crossed her mind that someone might happen upon them as they walked across the Downs, but somehow she could not bring herself to care enough to try to stop him. There was something about the way in which he kissed her that made Anna feel as if she was completely in his control, that she would do anything to please him.

It thrilled her, these unaccustomed feelings of submission, even while she worried about them. He had unfastened all the buttons of her dress now and he gazed down into her eyes before sitting up beside her.

Anna shivered slightly as a warm breeze kissed her naked skin, bringing goosebumps up on her flesh. Slowly, almost reverently, Dominic unclipped the fastening of her bra and peeled the separated cups away from her breasts. Then he slowly pulled her white cotton panties down, his fingertips brushing lightly along the golden fleece of her pubis before casting them aside.

Tracing a leisurely path across her body with the flat of his hand, Dominic kissed her, his tongue probing the inner recesses of her mouth, drawing a yearning response from hers. As his hand closed over one full breast, she stretched, like a cat in the sun, arching her back and flexing her toes.

He smiled, smoothing his hand down the side of her body and polishing her hipbone under his palm.

'Trust me,' he murmured, running the tip of his tongue along the inside of her lower lip which quivered under his touch.

Anna could feel the excitement curling in the pit of her stomach. This was crazy, totally insane!

'All right,' she mouthed.

His cool, firm lips brushed across her temples, his fingertips playing, featherlight, across her breasts and down to the gentle undulation of her stomach. The backs of his fingers stroked the golden curls at the apex of her thighs, teasing them until Anna's breath began to come in short, rapid gasps.

'Does that feel good?' he whispered, his warm, sweet breath tickling her ear.

Shivering in response, Anna closed her eyes and lay motionless, arms by her sides, squeezing her thighs tightly together in a fruitless attempt to ease the yearning ache caused by his careless caress. She could hear voices close by, carried on the soft breeze and wondered for a moment what she would do if someone came across them.

Dominic picked up her right hand and began to massage her fingers, moving slowly towards her knuckles which tingled under his light, circular caress. Bringing her hand up to his lips, he turned it so that he could press a kiss into her palm.

His lips were warm and dry, insistent as they repeated the small, sucking pressure in the centre of her open hand. Opening her eyes, Anna was caught by the intensity which shone in his and a piquant dart of lust shot through her belly. A sudden rush of moisture gathered between her legs, a ripe, expanding heaviness which made her sex lips swell and open in anticipation.

Dominic's eyes narrowed, crinkling attractively at the corners, and Anna gained the distinct impression that he knew. Feeling the damp warmth of his tongue pressing delicately into her tender skin, she had to suppress a moan of longing. She did not resist when he placed her hand gently on the soft mound at the base of her belly, enjoying the sensual feel of his palm stroking the back of her hand.

There was a distinct warmth coming from the folds of skin hidden below her hand, a simmering, hungry heat which embarrassed her. How could she be so licentious? It was some moments before she realised that Dominic was applying a gentle, but insistent pressure on the middle finger of her hand, so that it sank naturally into the hot, slippery flesh.

'No!'

Anna flushed as she whispered the denial, sure he knew how much she longed to touch herself, to stroke herself to orgasm under the wide open sky.

'Yes,' he whispered back, his lips trailing little, coaxing kisses down one side of her face.

Her need warred with her innate modesty, years of training which had told her it was a sin to touch herself there. She knew her eyes pleaded with him to help her draw back from the brink, yet he merely smiled gently down at her, his features shadowed by the bright sun which shone behind his head.

'I . . . I can't!'

Dominic said nothing, his eyes moving significantly down from her face to where her long, slender fingers were already moving inexorably deeper into the channels of flesh hidden between her thighs. Little sparks of pleasure travelled outward as her fingerpad moved more easily across her skin, its way eased by the slick moisture which seeped from her.

With a muffled groan of surrender, Anna closed her eyes and parted her legs, welcoming the kiss of the cool air which passed over her heated skin. She felt Dominic's lips against one raised knee, knew that he watched her pleasure herself as he rested his cheek gently against it.

Behind her closed eyelids, she imagined what he could see. The red, swollen folds of her sex lips opening beneath her fingers, her hot, wet vagina sucking her fingertip as she stroked and stirred it over her flesh. She was so wet she could feel her juices trickling down, over her perineum and into her bottom cleft before seeping into the itchy wool of the blanket.

It was too late to turn back now, the time for modesty had long passed. The heat running through her body had little to do with the warmth of the sun, everything to do with the sensations which were rioting through her.

Somehow, knowing that Dominic observed her so closely spurred her on, made her want to please him. The danger that someone might easily come across her, masturbating openly in the park, far from appalling her, added an extra frisson to her mounting excitement.

Using the first two fingers of her right hand now, she ran them either side of her inner labia, squeezing gently in a scissorlike movement on her swelling clitoris. Her breath began to come in short, shallow bursts as she spread her legs wider, reaching down with her other hand to hold herself open so that her right hand could attend exclusively to the tiny bud which had swelled to twice its normal size in response to her touch.

She wanted to beat that small, hard nub of flesh, to tap her fingertip against it until it felt as though it would burst, but a part of her held back. As if sensing that she was hanging on grimly to the last vestiges of her restraint, Dominic whispered encouragement in her ear, driving her wild with words of love and lust.

'Let it go, *chérie* . . . *maintenant* . . . let me see you come . . .'

All rational thought fled as the first jagged slivers of orgasm ripped through her. She didn't care any more, nothing mattered except her own physical gratification. Writhing against the blanket, Anna first plunged her index finger into the hot, sticky warmth of her vagina before smearing the honeyed juices up, over her straining clitoris.

Taking that tender morsel of flesh between two fingers, she made it stand proud of the surrounding flesh, a perfect target for the middle finger of her other hand. Transported to a different plane of consciousness, Anna tapped rhythmically on the straining nub.

'*Bien* . . . so beautiful . . . Anna, *je t'aime* . . .'

Dominic's voice was thick, his slurred words spurring her on until the rush of sensation suddenly peaked, taking her by surprise.

Squeezing her thighs tightly together, trapping her own hand between them, she raised her bottom up off the ground and gave in to the urge to cry out. Dominic immediately dipped his head, capturing her ecstatic cries in his mouth so that when, at last, the tumult began to subside, she was able to cling to him. Enclosing her trembling body in the warm safety of his embrace, he soothed her, kissing her hot face and murmuring endearments against her hair.

Anna leaned her head against his shoulder and allowed herself to be calmed by his rhythmic stroking of her hair and the low, pleasant cadence of his voice as he whispered to her. Never had she felt such intense plesaure at her own hands, never had she dreamed she could be capable of such total abandonment. It frightened her, this new found well of sensuality, yet it excited her more.

'I . . . I didn't want to do that,' she said tremulously when at last she could trust herself to speak.

She felt his lips curve into a smile as they rested on her temple.

'I know,' he whispered.

'. . . I didn't want to do it but . . . but I couldn't seem to stop myself . . .'

Dominic tilted her face so that he could look into her eyes. 'Don't think about it so much, Anna. You have within you the capacity for so much pleasure—'

'But Paul says . . .'

'Forget him – we will deal with his needs later. For now, put your trust in me. Will you do that, Anna?'

She gazed back at him and something in his eyes made the small thrill stir again, despite the satisfaction she had just enjoyed.

'Will you trust me?' he asked her again.

'Yes,' she whispered, surprising herself as she realised that she meant it. She *did* trust him, for all that he steered her into hitherto unknown territory.

Looking him directly in the eye, she repeated herself.

'I do trust you.'

Scanning her face, he saw the purity of that trust. And he smiled.

Chapter Five

ON THE SHORT drive home, Anna realised that, while she had reached the peak of sensual experience on the Downs, Dominic had done nothing except enjoy her pleasure. Glancing at him curiously, she saw that he was sitting beside her, perfectly relaxed, his dark eyes lazily taking in the beauty of the countryside through which they were driving.

She smiled to herself. Paul hated her to drive, never allowed her to do so when he was in the car, but this kind of chauvinism didn't seem to have occured to Dominic. As for remaining unfulfilled while she climbed the heights alone – well! Anna had an awful suspicion that her husband would rather die than submit to an impulse of such unselfishness.

'Something is funny?'

She felt Dominic's warm gaze on her and felt a blush steal into her cheeks.

'It's nothing,' she murmured, unable to resist the impulse to glance down at his lap, to see if he had been totally unaffected by all that had gone before.

Interpreting her gaze, he chuckled.

'We have the evening, no?'

His voice was low and smoky, sending shivers over her flesh. The innocuous phrase was heavy with hidden meaning, held such promise. Flashing him a look from beneath her lashes, she smiled.

'We do, don't we?'

At the back of her mind she supposed she should feel at least some guilt, some vestige of loyalty to Paul. But the thought of what *he* was doing, what he had done throughout their marriage, made her push such thoughts away.

Besides, the world Dominic was beginning to open up to her was so new, so exciting, Anna had little room in her thoughts for anything but their next encounter.

They completed the journey in companionable silence. As Anna pulled into the driveway and switched off the engine, Dominic turned to her.

'Would you like to go out tonight? Somewhere different, perhaps?'

Anna looked at him in surprise. When he had said they had the evening, she had supposed he meant they would spend it alone, more specifically, in bed.

'Well, I—'

She stopped abruptly as he unexpectedly leaned across the gear stick and kissed her.

'We will have fun, no?'

'No . . . yes,' she murmured, aching for more than that brief, warm fusion of his mouth with hers.

Inside the house, Dominic asked if he might make a telephone call to a friend.

'The place I am thinking of, we need a member to sign us in. Frankie will meet us there if I telephone.'

'Feel free. I'm going to take a bath – see you in about an hour?'

She left him to make his call, feeling slightly disappointed that she was not to have him all to herself. Still, she consoled herself as she turned on the taps, it would be interesting to see him amongst his friends.

Pouring in a generous amount of Estée Lauder bath milk, Anna closed her eyes and breathed in as the sweet smell of *Beautiful* filled the air. Pinning her hair up off her neck, she sank up to her chin into the hot, fragrant water and closed her eyes. Bliss!

Behind her closed eyelids, Anna replayed the scene on the Downs, remembering vividly every tiny detail. Floating her fingers just below the surface of the water, she let them rove to her thighs. Her skin felt soft and slippery, coated with a fine film of bath oil.

Shifting slightly, she created a small wave which rippled up her legs and broke gently against the mound of her pubis. Moving her fingers up the inside of her thigh, she stroked the golden curls of her mons before touching the warm, soft folds of flesh nestling within.

Remembering how she had touched herself before, she moved her fingertips gently, experimentally, up and down. Her labia were still swollen and puffy, slick with a heavier moisture than the bath water. It was easy to find her clitoris for it was still partially exposed. One touch of her finger and it escaped easily from under the protective hood of flesh which normally kept it from view.

'Ahh!' she sighed, enjoying the faint echo of the climax she had experienced on the Downs.

She had never masturbated to orgasm before and Anna wondered now if she could do it again, without Dominic's gentle encouragement. Her fingers slipped easily along the lightly oiled channels of her sex, their path made easier still by the silky bath water.

Her chest felt tight as, slowly but surely, little tendrils of pleasure began to curl outward from the heated centre of her, travelling to the tips of her fingers, the ends of her toes and tingling at the base of her skull.

Anna felt weightless, almost as if she were floating on the surface of the water. Opening herself wider, she eased her forefinger inside herself whilst, with the other hand, she stroked and teased the hard bud which seemed to strain towards her fingers.

The sensation of her slender finger filling her was not enough and she imagined it was replaced by a penis, a long, smooth, *anonymous* penis. Anna's eyes flew open as she realised that it didn't matter, in her fantasy, the male member could belong to any man, any man at all, so long as he could please her.

Whilst her mind was shocked, her fingers continued to stroke and pinch her sensitised flesh as if they had a life of their own. Groaning softly,

Anna let her subconscious take over.

The penis was moving more quickly now, withdrawing slowly, then plunging back into her with an unerring instinct for her pleasure. The water surged and slopped over the side of the bath as she flung her legs wider, using two fingers now, then three as she stimulated herself with rhythmic frenzy.

Rubbing furiously at her distended clitoris, she cried out as wave after wave of sensation crashed through her, leaving her breathless and perspiring. Even after the peak was reached, her body shook and shuddered as little aftershocks vibrated through it, pushing her beyond satisfaction, almost to the edge of pain.

When, at last, her breathing eased and the storm ebbed away, she slowly drew her knees together and lay back in the water, spent.

Anna smiled as she realised she had answered her question. She had only needed Dominic to show her that first, glorious time. From now on she had ecstasy at her fingertips – literally! She giggled. How wonderful it was that she could extract such delicious pleasure from her own body whenever and wherever she felt like it!

The water had begun to cool around her by the time Anna had regained sufficient energy to rouse herself. Towelling herself dry, she caught sight of herself in the mirror opposite the sink and her hands flew to her cheeks.

Her face was flushed, her eyes bright beneath sleepy lids. Even her mouth looked swollen, her lips red and puffy, much as she imagined her lower, more intimate lips would look. It would be obvious to anyone who looked at her exactly what she had been doing.

Thinking of Dominic waiting for her downstairs, Anna veered between mortification and satisfaction. A smile crept over her face as she decided she wouldn't be embarrassed. Why should she be? She felt good, better than she could ever remember feeling. And she knew that Dominic would be glad.

He had changed into black trousers and a lightweight black turtleneck. Narrowing his eyes, he ran them over her plain navy jersey dress with its high neck and long sleeves and raised his eyebrows.

'Why hide such a beautiful body, *chérie*?' he asked her bluntly.

Anna smiled seductively and walked slowly towards him, knowing that the fabric would cling to her body as she moved, emphasising every curve. Seeing the way the movement turned her plain dress into something far more alluring, Dominic smiled, taking her in his arms and kissing her on the forehead.

'*C'est bon,*' he admitted with a small, self-deprecating shrug of his shoulders.

Anna hid her smile against the warm cushion of his chest. Dominic's fingers swept along the curve of her cheek and grasped her chin. Raising her face to his, he scanned her bright eyes and slightly parted lips and she saw the recognition flare in his dark eyes. As she knew he would, he had guessed exactly what she had been doing!

'Shall we go?' he asked her, his voice unnaturally thick.

She nodded, tucking her hand companionably through the crook of his arm. Suddenly, she couldn't wait to go, to find out what else the day might hold.

They drove northwards, towards London. For a foreigner, Dominic had a clear idea of which roads to take and he directed her unerringly to a side street in Soho where several parking spaces were hidden behind what looked like a disused warehouse.

Feeding the meter, he watched as Anna locked up the car and walked towards him. She faltered slightly as she caught a look on his face that she didn't recognise. A remote, almost calculating expression which was so far removed from the warm, giving man she was coming to know that she felt compelled to whisper, 'Dominic?'

The sound of her voice wiped the look off his face and he smiled to her.

'Come,' he said, taking her by the hand, 'tonight I will show you something you have almost certainly never seen before. Okay?'

He waited, as if giving her the chance to turn back, to go home. But Anna didn't want to go home. Her curiosity provoked, she was eager to see this thing he promised to show her, sure it could only add to the lessons in sensuality he had already taught her.

'Okay,' she nodded.

They turned into another side street, then out on to a noisier, busier thoroughfare. Anna's eyes popped as they walked past the neon-bright strip joints, some with scantily clad girls sitting behind glass panels, glowing with boredom. *Girls, Girls,*

Girls! proclaimed an especially lurid sign across the road and Anna was amazed to see the number of customers streaming in, and out, of the place.

'Where *are* we going?' she asked Dominic after a few minutes' walk.

'Patience, *ma chérie*, it isn't far. See – there is Frankie.'

His pace quickened and Anna had to lengthen her stride to keep up with him. Scanning the people ahead of them, she couldn't see anyone with whom she would have thought Dominic to be friendly. She quickly realised why when he stopped and she saw that Frankie was a girl. A rather beautiful girl.

'Frankie!'

Dominic took her in his arms and kissed her twice on each cheek. A sensation very close to pain sliced through Anna's chest, taking her by surprise. She didn't like the way Dominic was touching the girl, in so familiar a way that it was obvious that they were more, much more than 'good friends'.

Recognising the feeling as jealousy, Anna was appalled. She had no claim on Dominic, had only just met him, she had no right to feel this way! Carefully keeping her expression neutral, she smiled as Dominic introduced her.

'Anna, this is Francine – Frankie to her friends. Frankie, Anna is my temporary landlady, as well as a very good friend,' he smiled.

Frankie held out her hand.

'I am very pleased to meet you, Anna.'

The girl was as French as Dominic, her voice low and husky, naturally seductive.

'Likewise,' Anna murmured politely.

Frankie turned back to Dominic then, giving Anna the opportunity to look at her more closely. She was the same height as her, though slighter, her figure being shown to perfect advantage by the clinging red knit dress she was wearing. It moulded the generous swell of her breasts before moving in with her body to the fetching indentation of her waist. Her hips, though not large, were rounded, giving her a traditional hourglass figure.

Frankie's hair, as dark as Anna's was fair, was long and straight, falling loose in a glossy black curtain to her waist. Her olive-toned skin was flawless and smooth, her unusual, topaz-coloured eyes slanted slightly, giving her a catlike appearance. A small, straight nose sat above a generous mouth, her soft lips painted red to match her dress.

She must have felt Anna's gaze on her, for she turned her head slightly whilst talking to Dominic and caught Anna's eye. Embarrassed to have been caught staring, Anna smiled sheepishly. A slow, almost seductive smile spread over Frankie's face as her eyes narrowed hypnotically, holding Anna's gaze.

Anna felt uncomfortable, though she couldn't for the life of her think why. Staring back at Frankie unblinkingly, she was conscious of relief when the other girl broke eye contact. Only then did she realise she had been holding her breath, for it rushed through her parted lips on a sigh.

Frankie and Dominic exchanged a look that Anna could not interpret. Slipping his arm possessively round Anna's waist, Dominic smiled his whimsical, slightly lop-sided smile at her.

'Shall we go inside?' he asked her.

Anna nodded and the three of them stepped through the black-painted glass into the foyer of the club. Waiting nervously while Frankie went to the desk to sign them in, Anna was glad of Dominic's warm fingers slipping beneath her hair to cup the nape of her neck.

'Relax, *chérie*,' he murmured, close to her ear, 'you are too tense, no?'

His long, clever fingers squeezed the taut muscles of her neck and Anna leaned into him, closing her eyes briefly against the sudden, unexpected rush of desire she experienced as his strong, lean body was pressed against hers.

It was as though his mere physical nearness was enough to arouse her. The more she had of him, the more she wanted and at once she wished fervently that they had stayed at home, alone.

Dominic's lips brushed over the top of her ear, his warm breath tickling across its folds. Shivering, Anna turned her face slightly towards his, yearning for the touch of his mouth on hers. Planting a small, chaste kiss at the corner of her mouth, it seemed he could not resist darting out his tongue and insinuating the tip between her trembling lips.

'Ready?'

Anna moved guiltily away as Frankie re-joined them. Anna found herself walking between the two with Frankie's lush feminine curves as close as the harder, more masculine planes of Dominic's body.

The room into which they were shown was dimly lit by dozens of candles held in iron sconces around the walls. A circular area of floor space had been cleared, a spotlight shining from the ceiling picking out a black velvet covered couch in the centre of the room. All around it, white shrouded tables with miniature candelabra seated the patrons in twos and fours, the flickering candles lighting up their faces in an almost ethereal glow.

Frankie led them to a table set for three beside the stage. As they sat down, Dominic between the two women, a dark-suited waiter appeared noiselessly at their table and passed them each a menu. Frankie waved them away.

'Oysters to start, *s'il vous plaît*, Tomas, followed by the veal in cream and white wine. Trust me, Anna,' she said with a smile as Anna began to protest, 'this you will enjoy.'

Trust me. That is what Dominic had said to her, in the beginning. Glancing at him, Anna saw he was smiling, though the expression in his dark eyes was inscrutable. He nodded at her, urging her to accept Frankie's choice, and Anna felt obliged to do so.

'*Bon*. Some champagne too, Tomas!' Frankie looked inordinately pleased by Anna's capitulation.

Anna was left with the uncomfortable feeling that there was more at stake than her freedom to choose the food she ate. Which was a ridiculous thing to think, she told herself, Frankie was only being polite.

Looking around her, she saw that most of their

fellow diners were already eating and only a low murmur of conversation could be heard above the classical music being piped through the room. There was an almost tangible air of suppressed excitement in the room, a sense of expectation which had Anna intrigued.

Her attention was abruptly dragged back to her companions as she realised that they were talking about her.

'She is very beautiful, Dominic, you have excellent taste.'

'Of course, *chérie* – haven't I always?'

A small, complicit smile passed between them, leaving Anna in no doubt that they were, or had been lovers. She felt the heat seep under her skin as they continued to discuss her as if she wasn't there.

'She looks so innocent! Surely she cannot be that . . . unknowing?' Frankie chuckled softly.

Dominic glanced at Anna, his dark eyes sparkling with amusement. Seeing her distress, he caught hold of her hand under the table and lifted it to his lips. Holding her gaze, he replied.

'She is quite unique, *n'est-ce pas*? A perfect pupil.'

Anna felt the familiar stirring in her womb as his low, husky voice caressed her ears, even though she hated being discussed like this. She didn't even know the other girl, for goodness sake; she didn't like the way she seemed to feel herself entitled to be privy to her most intimate secrets.

Catching her eye, Anna realised that Frankie knew how she felt all too well and that somehow, she was amused by it. Though not in an unpleasant way, there was something almost sisterly in the way she was smiling at her now. Anna looked away, confused.

The champagne arrived and was opened with a discreet *pop* beside them. Anna watched the ebullient, pale gold liquid hiss and fizz in her glass rather than look at Frankie. Dutifully, she raised her glass and chinked it against theirs before gulping it down, unwisely, for the bubbles rushed down her throat and up her nose, making her cough.

Dominic patted her on the back.

'Slowly, *ma chérie*, we have the whole night ahead of us.'

Anna smiled sheepishly at him, relaxing a little.

Their oysters arrived and Anna found her concentration fully taken up with eating them from their shells. She found she liked the way they slipped effortlessly down her throat and she wondered whether their reputation as an aphrodisiac was real or a myth. Not that she'd needed an aphrodisiac since Dominic strode into her life.

They were halfway through their main course, which was as delicious as Frankie had promised it would be, when the piped music abruptly stopped. A buzz of excited anticipation ran round the room as a man took his place at a piano which Anna hadn't noticed, tucked away as it was in the corner of the room, and began to play.

Suddenly, the lights around the floor stage went up and a woman appeared at the centre, as if from nowhere and began to sing.

'*Start spreading the news, I'm leaving today, I want*

to be a part of it, New York, New York . . .'

Anna watched in surprise as the woman belted out the old song in a voice fit for the West End. She was wearing a long, pink skirt with a heavily sequinned tunic which skimmed her figure. High, high heels peeked from beneath the skirt, and she towered above the audience, her demeanour challenging, dominating those who watched her.

Her heavily made-up face was framed by several sculpted brown curls which protruded from the pink, sequin-covered skull cap adorned with pink feathers she wore. Anna wasn't sure what she had expected, but it certainly wasn't this glittering array of sequins and feathers swaying in time to the kind of song her mother sang whilst doing the dishes. Somehow it seemed bizarre.

'Who is it?' she whispered to Dominic.

'Her name is Fleuris. She can sing, no?'

He chuckled at her bemused expression, her eyes widening as, high kicking her way to a crescendo, Fleuris cast her long skirt aside to reveal thigh high leather boots and sturdy-looking suspenders. Black leather knickers completed the look, moulding her pubis and buttocks so closely that they managed to look obscene.

The tempo changed, the lights switching to blue and green and red, striping the stage around her as she dropped her voice an octave and began to croon, *'See me, feel me . . .'*

This was more what Anna had expected! As Fleuris arched her back and unclipped her tunic, a collective sigh rose up from the audience. She was wearing what Anna could only describe to herself as a halter; thin strips of leather studded with little silver cones which criss-crossed her breasts and fastened around her neck and waist. As she moved, her large, reddened nipples peeked through the strips of leather before being hidden again.

Glancing sideways at Dominic, through her lashes, Anna saw that he was watching the dancer intently, his eyes narrowed. That he was enjoying the display was plain; she could sense his tension in the way he held himself, keeping his arousal in check.

Maybe he would like her to dance for him, like this? Anna felt a thrill of anticipation as she imagined herself writhing, half naked, to music for Dominic's pleasure . . . could she do it? She watched the dancer more closely, deciding she would try first in the privacy of her own room.

By the end of the song, Fleuris had shaken off the closely-fitting skull cap and her long brown hair swept the floor at her feet as she bent almost double, from the waist, her face hidden from view as she gasped the final few bars of the song.

Straightening, she threw back her hair and looked imperiously around the room at the applauding audience, fists on hips, microphone cast carelessly aside. She looked magnificent, her full breasts heaving beneath their constricting restraint, her hair awry and her face flushed with exertion.

Anna's heart almost skipped a beat as the dancer suddenly caught her eye and she recognised the look she was giving her. It was lustful, ravenously so and Anna squirmed in her seat. She felt Dominic's warm hand on her knee and covered it with her own, glad that he was with her.

The woman on the stage smiled down at her, baring her teeth so that the smile turned almost into a snarl. Then the stage was filled with swirling smoke and loud, thudding music filled the air as four, no five dancers burst on to the stage and swarmed around her.

Three women, two men, they lifted her effortlessly between them and bore her off to the black velvet couch where she sprawled, as if in a trance.

'What's happening?'

Dominic placed a finger against her mouth as she whispered to him and nodded towards the couch, indicating that she should watch. The female dancers were all wearing metallic silver bikinis, their arms and legs bare. The two men wore nothing but black leather G-strings which did little to conceal their state of arousal. Together they all ran their hands over Fleuris' prone body, stroking, pinching, feeling every inch of her.

Gone was the almost regal, proud dominatrix; Fleuris was now reduced to an object of pleasure, a vehicle for the gratification of the audience.

The atmosphere in the room was electric now, and Anna could feel the tension all around her as, after a few minutes of this frenzied groping, the dancers helped Fleuris to her feet. The two men each took an arm, urging her forward so that she was centre stage.

The woman's face was set in lines of almost beatific suffering, her eyes, black as coals, burning with desire. Anna felt a jolt of recognition as she stared at her eyes. She *knew* how she felt, had herself felt the same, desperate need for release from the first time Dominic had shown her what sex could be about.

A hush descended over the room as the music changed tempo, became slow and dreamy. An audible gasp came from the audience as one of the female dancers peeled off the woman's leather panties and held them to her nose, inhaling deeply before offering them to one of the others. One by one they sniffed the woman's panties, as if sharing in some secret ritual.

Fleuris moaned softly, not quite in protest as, at last, they were cast aside and one of the girls began to caress her thighs. Supported on either side by the two men, she submitted to the girl's bold caresses, arching her back and moaning louder when she tangled her fingers in the dark mass of pubic hair at the apex of her thighs.

Anna's throat felt dry as the girl began to open her, careful not to obscure the view of the audience, all of whose eyes were riveted on the small purse of swollen, red flesh now revealed. Never having seen another woman so intimately revealed, Anna stared as hard as anyone, fascinated by the intricate topography of Fleuris' vulva.

Under the harsh glare of the stage lights, her labia glistened with the moisture of arousal as the girl ran her fingertip along the grooves, carefully separating and tantalising each fold of flesh. It was as if she was preparing her, readying her for whatever it was that would come next.

Anna could feel tension knotting in her stomach as she tried to think what that could be.

Was she to be fucked on stage, in front of them all? She was appalled and excited by the idea in equal measure, shifting forward slightly in her seat as she realised that, so subtly it was almost imperceptible, the mood had changed.

The music was quieter now, so quiet in fact that she could hear Fleuris' heavy breathing. The woman was almost panting, so deeply came her breaths, and the expression on her face had glazed so that she probably didn't know where she was, or what she was doing.

Slowly, showily, the two men turned her around, so that her back was to most of the audience. One of them placed a hand on the back of her head and coaxed her to bend over, pushing her bottom in the air, her constricted breasts hanging over the floor.

One of the girls deftly unclipped the fastenings of the halter and it fell away. The woman's large breasts swung free, eliciting a muted cheer from a man in the audience. Anna watched, mesmerised, as another girl got down on her knees and took one reddened teat into her mouth. Her cheeks bulged as she sucked and squeezed.

The woman's head moved from side to side as a second girl took her other breast and began to lick and suck, her eyes closed as if in ecstasy.

Meanwhile, the third girl stroked her bottom, urging her to stand with her feet wider apart, to bend her knees slightly so that her bottom cheeks gaped apart. Anna could see the tight, puckered entrance to her body, her vulva open and exposed beneath it like a red, ripe fruit, shining with moisture.

She gasped as the third girl suddenly plunged her forefinger inside the woman's vagina, whilst one of the men reached forward and held her labia apart so that audience could see more clearly what was happening. Withdrawing her finger, the girl held it up so that the watchers could see the juices glistening on her finger. Then she offered it to one of the girls on the floor who immediately left the breast to which she had been attending and lapped at her colleague's finger greedily, licking it clean.

Anna was only vaguely aware of the muted chant which had begun to their left where four young men sat, pressing forward in their seats, their eyes bright and lustful.

'Do it to her, do it to her, do it to her . . .'

Snapping her attention back to the floor show, Anna realised at last what was going to happen. The third girl disappeared momentarily, returning with a long, black object, from which hung several strips of leather. And she realised that Fleuris was about to be whipped.

Stunned, Anna tried to say that she couldn't watch, she wanted to go home – now! But the words would not force themselves through her dry throat, her eyes would not move from the scene before her.

And as she felt the familiar, damp warmth seep into her briefs, she realised that she didn't want to go at all. She wanted to stay right here and watch another woman being whipped purely for the delight of the people who watched.

Anna whimpered softly as she felt Dominic's hand creep further up her leg. God, she needed him to touch her *there*, wanted him to feel how much she was enjoying the spectacle before her. Fleuris was rotating her hips now, whether in protest or to tempt the girl now making a great show of cracking the whip on the floor, Anna could not tell.

The smell of sex was heavy in the air, the scent of arousal, both male and female, combining to create a heady, intoxicating aroma. Anna felt hot, beads of perspiration pushing through the pores of her skin all over her body. She couldn't breathe properly, her entire attention was fixed on the woman in front of her and the five dancers who were still tormenting her.

Dominic's fingers had breached the tight elastic of her knickers now and were moving inexorably towards the heated channel of her sex. Anna moaned as his fingertips brushed tantalisingly over the hard button of her clitoris, seeking the moisture which had gathered in the lip of her vagina.

They didn't look at each other, not even when Anna, impatient with the restriction imposed by her underwear, wriggled out of her briefs and left them lying around one ankle. Dominic placed his whole hand over her vulva and squeezed, as if in approval, before going back to the serious business of making her come.

The girl with the whip held the handle against the entrance to Fleuris' body and, after pausing theatrically, eased it in. The audience went wild as it sank in up to the hilt and Fleuris wiggled her hips to show off the strips of leather protruding like a tail from her bulging vagina.

The men on the table to Anna's left who had called out earlier had all unzipped their trousers and were openly masturbating, two of them doing the favour for each other. Anna guessed that, if she could drag her eyes away from Fleuris for long enough, she would see that they weren't the only ones. But she couldn't stop watching, her pulse rate quickening still more.

Increasing the pressure of his fingers against the moisture-slick folds of her innermost flesh, Dominic twirled his fingertip around the hard nub of flesh which was already beginning to pulse and throb. Anna watched, mesmerised, as the whip was withdrawn from Fleuris' body and held up for the audience to see. It gleamed in the spotlight, glistening with the secretions from Fleuris' body.

Anna's breath hurt in her chest as the girl transferred the handle of the whip to her fist and stood back a little. It seemed as if the entire audience held their breath as she flicked it and the split end cracked across the woman's up-turned buttocks.

'Noooo!'

Fleuris' anguished cry, more sob than yell, filled the air and the audience gave a collective groan. Anna's hips jerked as Dominic took her clitoris between his finger and thumb and pinched it, hard, wringing her climax from her.

Orgiastic cries went up all around the room as the audience exploded into what seemed to Anna to be the biggest mutual climax possible. Panting, she rocked her pelvis on Dominic's hand until she was spent.

Only then did she realise that the floor show had ended, the dancers and the singer had melted away under cover of the excess of sexual excitement and the stage was now in darkness. She turned to Dominic, flushed and sated, to find he was stroking Frankie's hair.

Feeling Anna's eyes on her, Frankie raised her face to look at her. One look at the other girl's face told Anna that she too had just experienced orgasm. Her beautiful, topaz eyes were glazed and unfocussed and a soft tinge of pink showed under the flawless olive complexion.

Realising that Dominic must have been masturbating her at the same time as he was her, Anna was filled with admiration. Such concentration!

Frankie smiled lazily at her and Anna realised with a start that she didn't mind. Slipping her hand under the table, she squeezed his thigh, whilst over the table, she held Frankie's eye. Knowing how the other girl was feeling, she smiled, a tingle of sisterly empathy running through her as Frankie's soft mouth widened into a small, almost conspiratorial smile.

Watching them, Dominic sighed in contentment, leaning forward to pour more champagne.

Chapter Six

TO ANNA'S SURPRISE, Dominic announced it was time to leave soon after. She would have liked to have stayed, to see what other entertainments the club had to offer that evening, but Dominic's dark eyes were implacable.

Frowning, Anna turned to Frankie.

'It's been lovely meeting you, Francine,' she told the other woman, realising as she did so that she meant every word.

'Please – call me Frankie since we are to be friends.'

She smiled at Anna as her fingertip trailed lazily down the side of Dominic's face. Anna watched, mesmerised, as Dominic turned his head and captured one perfectly manicured fingertip between his lips. Frankie's eyes closed momentarily as he nipped it, the smile never leaving her face. Anna's stomach cramped with the desire she knew the other woman felt and, suddenly, she was just as eager as Dominic to head for home.

He was silent as they walked briskly back

towards the car. The city streets were streaked with rain, the pavement glittering black beneath their feet. There was a heavy, oppressive tension in the air, making her feel hot and breathless as she kept pace with Dominic.

'May I drive your car?' he asked unexpectedly as they reached it.

'If you like – I think I'm a bit close to the limit after all that champagne.'

He smiled and caught the keys she threw at him over the bonnet.

'You like champagne, no?'

Anna slipped into the passenger seat, arranging her long skirt demurely around her.

'I don't have it often. You don't know you like something until you try it, do you?'

Their eyes met in the darkened interior of the car and Anna held her breath, awestruck by the sudden tension hanging in the air between them. He was so close, she could see the light of a nearby streetlamp reflected in his pupils, smell the clean, tangy scent of his skin.

He stared at her, unsmiling, unblinking, for what seemed like an age. Anna felt as though something was melting inside her body, her arms and legs grew hot and heavy, the hidden places between her thighs swelling and moistening in anticipation.

The disappointment was acute when he suddenly turned away and switched on the engine.

They drove five, ten, twelve miles, gradually leaving the capital behind them and driving on through the suburbs. Stark urban streets melted into leafy avenues as the rain became heavier, coming down in sheets so that the windscreen wipers were finding it difficult to cope with the deluge.

Sensibly, Dominic pulled over to wait for the torrent to ease. As far as Anna could see, they were parked outside a row of sturdy nineteen-twenties semis. She couldn't see much through the driving rain, but she could imagine what the neighbourhood was like – all the houses would be tastefully set back from the road, their well maintained railings and gates keeping out unwanted visitors, their carefully tended front gardens trimmed and manicured.

She turned her head as she felt Dominic's eyes on her again. His expression was stiff, forbidding and at once the atmosphere inside the car was as heavy as the air outside it.

'Get in the back.'

Anna blinked, unable to believe her ears. No 'please', no hint of suggestion, just one, stark order. *Get in the back*.

She had to let the seat tilt back to enable her to obey him without getting out of the car and getting soaked to the skin. Even then it was a squeeze and she had to kick off her shoes and pull her dress up above her knees in order to clamber across.

She was breathing heavily by the time she reached the back seat. Wondering what kind of sight she presented to Dominic, hot and perspiring, her hair escaping from its pins and falling in damp tendrils around her face. She gazed at him expectantly.

Somehow, in spite of his extra height, he managed to climb into the back of the small car far more quickly and gracefully than she had done. Fighting down a growing feeling of claustrophobia, Anna let out her pent-up breath in a long sigh and leaned towards him.

He did not kiss her as she had expected. Instead, he reached down and curled his fingers around the hem of her dress and bunched it round her waist. The backs of his knuckles grazed over her still damp panties as he sought the elastic at her waist.

'Turn around.'

Anna did as she was asked with difficulty, raising up her buttocks so that he could remove her briefs. Her face was pressed up against the window and the glass felt cool against her cheek. Twisting her head round, she watched as Dominic unzipped his trousers, releasing his swollen cock into his hand.

She licked her lips, swallowing hard to lubricate her dry throat. It looked so big, so near to explosion and suddenly she couldn't wait to have it inside her, to feel it sliding against the silkily abrasive walls of her sex.

His eyes glittered in the darkness as he reached for her, holding her at the waist with his hands and pulling her down so that she was virtually sitting on his lap. She felt the bulbous cock head nudge insistently at the entrance to her body, felt herself open and enclose him.

Sinking slowly down on to his lap, Anna held on to the head-rest of the passenger seat for support. Her bottom touched his belly as his cock hit home, touching the neck of her womb with a small, familiar kiss.

Anna threw back her head, feeling her hair fall out of its pins and stream down her back, brushing his face. Her body welcomed him, sheathing his aggressive male member, enclosing it, loving it. Revelling in her control, she lifted her buttocks, raising herself up until he almost slipped out of her, then plunged back down again, recapturing his hard flesh.

The rain played in a cacophonous symphony against the roof of the car, the windows awash with a continuous downpour as they raced towards their mutual peak. Anna could feel the car rocking with them as she sensed when to move more quickly. Squeezing her vaginal muscles tightly, she forced a low, ecstatic groan from him. The small sound excited her beyond reason, speeding her onward towards her own climax.

Reaching down, she rubbed her clitoris with her finger pad, moving it round and round in time to the now frantic thrust of her hips. Dominic cried out as he came, pumping his seed into her as if from a bottomless well, his fingers digging almost painfully into the soft flesh of her waist.

Ripples of pleasure radiated out from the tiny button of pleasure now caught between their bodies. Moving her head from side to side, Anna brushed his face with her hair, absorbing the faint trembling of his body against her back as he slowly descended from that higher plane.

Slowly, they peeled apart and he helped her to

rearrange her clothes. To Anna's surprise, she saw that at some point during their frenzied coupling the rain had stopped. As she climbed awkwardly across the seats to the passenger side, a movement caught her eye.

At the side of the road, mere feet away from the place where they had parked, there was a bus stop. An old-fashioned, wooden shelter, from which there now emerged three young men who gaped openly at her as she slid into her seat and fastened her seatbelt.

'Oh my God!' Anna whispered. 'Dominic – they're coming over – start the car for God's sake!'

He seemed to take an age to fire the engine and draw sedately away, an age in which all kinds of awful things flew through Anna's mind. The trio were in their late teens or early twenties, clearly on their way home after a night on the town. They might be drunk, or high on God knew what . . . and they'd watched her car rock as she and Dominic . . .

'Relax, *chérie*, you're quite safe,' Dominic said as they sped through the night.

'Dammit, Dominic, it isn't funny . . .'

She caught his eye and collapsed into fits of giggles.

That night as they lay in bed, he seemed content to simply hold her as they both drifted into sleep. If only, she thought as his breathing became deep and even beside her, if only it could always be like this . . . turning her face so that her cheek was pressed against the warm, bare skin of his chest, she closed her eyes and sighed.

*

'That's the third time this morning you've not heard what I've said,' Alan pointed out as Anna looked blankly at him the next day.

'I'm sorry, Alan, I'm just not with it today.'

'Are you sure you feel all right? You look a bit peaky to me.'

Anna felt herself blush as Alan peered shortsightedly at her. Whatever would he think if he could read her mind? She had to pull herself together and stop allowing thoughts of Dominic to intrude on the ordinary, mundane fabric of her day. Taking a deep breath, she consciously pulled herself together and began to apologise. 'I—'

'How are you feeling now, Ann-a? I have been worried about you.'

Anna swung round on her office chair as Dominic's voice came from behind her. The twinkle in his eye told her that he had overheard Alan's concerned enquiry, the slight twitch of his lips signalling his amusement at her distraction and his awareness of its cause.

Alan, however, took Dominic's comment at face value, apparently oblivious to his blatant manipulation. Turning back to Anna, he frowned. 'Have you been ill?'

'I thought she should stay away from work this morning, Alan,' Dominic said before Anna could answer, 'but she seemed to think she was . . . what is the word? *Indispensable*, no?'

Alan blew air between his lips in an impatient exclamation which Anna knew well. When he spoke, his tone was mildly scolding, making Anna feel like a small child.

'That doesn't surprise me at all, the girl works

far too hard as it is. Pick up your things, Anna and take yourself off home. For goodness sake, girl, you're no good to me here if you're feeling half dead!'

Anna gaped in astonishment at the two men. Quite apart from being discussed as if she was not in the room, she wasn't sure that she liked having them dictate to her. Besides, she felt perfectly well. If she was pale, it was only due to the lack of sleep she had endured lately . . . she felt the colour flood her cheeks as she thought of the reason why she had been sleeping so little since Dominic arrived.

Still, she couldn't possibly take advantage of Alan like this and, Dominic or no Dominic, she was going to come clean.

'Allow me to drive you,' Dominic offered, obviously aware that she was about to profess to feeling her usual hale and hearty self.

'That won't be necessary. Besides, haven't you got a lecture this afternoon?'

'Now I know you're ill,' Alan remarked acidly. 'You typed the memo moving it forward to this morning yourself earlier in the week.'

Looking from Alan's concerned face to the mischievous twinkle in Dominic's eyes, Anna saw that she was beaten.

'All right,' she sighed, 'if you insist, I'll go home.'

'Take the rest of the week off,' Alan directed magnanimously.

'Oh well, if I'm *that* dispensable,' she laughed, only half in jest. 'What was all that about?' she asked Dominic as he hurried her across the car park.

Taking her keys from her, he unlocked her car and opened the passenger door for her.

'I wanted you all to myself,' he grinned almost boyishly at her across the roof of the car and Anna's stomach lurched.

She slid slowly into her seat and took her time fastening her seatbelt, trying to control the sudden trembling of her hands. Inevitably, Dominic's warm fingers closed over hers and he slid the buckle effortlessly into its housing.

'I've never played hookey from work before,' she admitted in an attempt to lighten the atmosphere.

"Ookey?' he raised an eyebrow quizzically at her and she laughed.

'Never mind. Well, start the engine, Dominic, or Alan will wonder what's going on.'

He smiled slightly and started the car, saying casually as he manoeuvred out of the car park, 'Frankie invited us to stay with her for a few days. Now that you are so ill, perhaps you would like for me to accept?'

His tone was too casual, too nonchalant, and Anna stiffened. Butterflies beat their wings against the inside of her stomach as a picture of Dominic sucking on the tip of Francine's long, elegant fingers sprang into her mind. Excitement cramped in her belly.

'That would be nice,' she said, her voice barely more than a whisper.

Glancing at Dominic from the corner of her eye, she watched his capable hands on the steering wheel and remembered the feel of them on her body. They were clever, sensitive hands, seeking out every tender groove and furrow, sometimes loving, sometimes merely compelling, but always unerringly accurate.

Did those hands know the contours of Francine's body as well as they knew hers? A dart of jealousy pierced through her, threaded through with something else, an emotion Anna could not identify, but which thrilled her to the core. Recalling Francine's lazy, catlike regard, her pulse quickened.

Settling back into her seat, she realised that a stay with Frankie would be no ordinary house party. Her agreement to go would extend to far more than the usual responsibilities of a guest. Did Dominic realise how big a leap into the unknown this was for her? Her eyes flickered towards him uncertainly.

He must have felt her covert regard, for he turned his head and smiled at her. Lifting one hand from the steering wheel he covered hers. His touch felt so warm, so *familiar*. Whatever this visit held in store, Dominic would be with her. She trusted him, didn't she?

He smiled at her again, a smile of such luminosity that it lit up his face. Anna felt the excitement travel through her limbs, chasing away every flicker of doubt, of apprehension.

Her lips curved into a small smile of anticipation as she settled her head back on the seat and closed her eyes.

Chapter Seven

FRANCINE'S HOUSE WAS nothing like Anna had expected it to be. Dazzled, perhaps, by the Frenchwoman's polished elegance, she supposed she had expected a modern penthouse somewhere in the reclaimed Docklands or similar. Nothing prepared her for the pretty, thatched cottage hidden away at the end of a long lane in a small village.

'It was left to me by my English *grand-mère*,' Frankie explained, seeing Anna looking curiously about her.

Uncomfortable at having been caught staring, Anna smiled and followed Frankie inside. The house was warm and welcoming, spotlessly clean with sparkling, many paned windows, most of which had a vase of fresh flowers on the sill. Pot pourri perfumed the air together with, unbelievably, a delicious aroma wafting in from the kitchen. She hadn't expected Francine to be quite so . . . *domesticated*!

'You've arrived just on time – dinner is almost ready!'

Anna turned to see Frankie walking into the low ceilinged living-room, her arm slipped casually through Dominic's. She was wearing a pair of slim fitting, stonewashed jeans and a navy blue ribbed top which clung to her small breasts, emphasising the perfection of their shape. Her long, dark hair fell loose down her back, caught over each ear with a small, round, child's hairslide. On any other woman, the adornment would have looked affected, on Francine it was merely charming. Her slanted topaz-yellow eyes sparkled at Anna without a hint of jealousy. Her smile was wide and genuine and Anna warmed to her, unaware until that moment of how tense she had been on the journey down.

Dominic poured them all a drink and sat beside Anna on the comfortable sofa while Frankie went to see to dinner.

'I wish she'd let me help,' Anna fretted when they were alone.

Dominic smiled and touched his glass against hers.

'Like most things Frankie does she likes to work alone. She cooks like a professional.' He kissed the first two fingers of his right hand for emphasis. 'She'll have everything under control.'

Anna held his gaze as they both sipped from their wine glasses. He spoke of Francine with such warmth, such obvious affection. Anna felt as though she ought to feel jealous, yet there wasn't so much of a flicker of that emotion running through her. There was curiosity, a definite excitement, but no envy.

There was no time to marvel at the realisation,

for Frankie reappeared and announced that dinner was ready. She showed them into a charming dining-room, dominated by an oval rosewood table. It was set with fine crystal, solid silver and bone china. At the end of the room were French windows looking out on to the garden.

'What a lovely view to have over breakfast!' Anna exclaimed as she looked out on to an abundance of roses.

'Yes,' Francine smiled, coming up behind Anna and laying a casual hand on her shoulder. 'In the mornings I watch the birds and sometimes there are squirrels and hedgehogs.'

Anna supposed she made the right noises in reply for the conversation continued around her. All she could think about was the feel of Frankie's hand on her shoulder. Even now, after the other woman had moved away, Anna could feel the warmth of her skin through the thin fabric of her blouse and was shocked by her reaction. Desire didn't seem to be an appropriate response to another woman's touch.

'If you'd like to sit here, Anna?'

Anna shook herself as she realised that Frankie was talking to her.

'Oh . . . thank you!'

She took her place between the two of them and watched as Dominic poured her another glass of wine. She couldn't remember finishing the first and she made a mental note to drink this one more slowly.

Dinner was delicious.

'I've had coq au vin before, but it never tasted like this!' she told Frankie.

Francine smiled. 'It has to be cooked by someone French!' she declared, po-faced.

The light in the garden outside faded fast, leaving them dependent on the flickering light of the candles on the table. Gentle, melodious music seeped through the room from an unidentifiable source, unobtrusive yet poignant.

Anna could smell Francine's musky perfume as she leaned across to clear their plates. It mingled with Dominic's more familiar, inherently masculine scent which enclosed her when he leaned over her to top up her glass. She felt drowsy, made sleepy by the combination of their long drive down, rich food and a surfeit of wine.

The light, lime mousse was fluffy on her tongue, slipping down effortlessly as she let the desultory conversation ebb and flow around her. No one seemed to mind that she did not contribute much. Dominic's thigh was warm against hers under the table, his foot playing with hers as they ate. At last they all sat back in their seats, replete.

'Why don't we go through to the living-room – you look tired, Anna?'

Anna smiled ruefully at Francine's concern.

'I'm sorry – does it show that much?'

Dominic chuckled softly. 'Maybe you are not feeling so well after all?'

'That would serve me right, wouldn't it?' she smiled a little ruefully. 'I feel fine, just a little sleepy, that's all.'

'Well, you two go and sit down, I'll bring the coffee through.'

'Oh, but I must help to clear the table—'

'No, you go with Dominic,' Frankie interrupted her firmly. 'It won't take me long.'

Dominic sank with her on to the floral sofa and wasted no time in taking her in his arms. His breath was sweet, redolent of red wine and the faint echo of lime. The kiss sent tiny tremors of delight feathering up and down Anna's spine.

'No,' she protested reluctantly, holding him off with her palms against his chest.

'*Non?*'

'It . . . doesn't seem right, not in Francine's house . . .' she trailed off, aware that the words weren't coming out as she had intended they should.

She felt the rumble of Dominic's laughter vibrating under her hands.

'Frankie will not mind, *chérie*,' he whispered, 'I have been wanting to kiss you all through dinner.'

This time when his lips closed over hers, Anna allowed herself to respond for a few minutes more, springing away from him as she heard Frankie's light footfall outside the door.

The other girl came in laden down with a coffee tray and Dominic went to help her. Her knowing smile told Anna that she had missed nothing and she blushed.

The coffee was dark and bitter, yet quite delicious. Frankie put on some more music and the three of them settled down in the warm, comfortable room, Anna and Dominic on the sofa, Francine sitting on the sheepskin rug by the fire, her long, slender legs curled under her.

Anna felt warm and happy, but so, so weary.

Leaning her head against Dominic's shoulder, she allowed her eyelids to close, sure no one would mind if she napped, just for a few minutes . . .

When she awoke she was lying full length on the sofa. Someone had covered her with a quilt and eased a cushion under her head so that she felt stiff, but not uncomfortably so. The sky outside the uncurtained window was pitch black, the shadows in the room illuminated by a single lamp left burning by the fireside.

Disorientated, Anna sat up and ran her fingers through her hair. It felt tangled, adding to her sense of dishevelment. She couldn't remember where she had put her bag. Hadn't Dominic taken it upstairs for her when they first arrived?

Swinging her legs over the side of the sofa, she stretched, raising her arms above her head and loosening her cramped shoulder muscles. Standing up, she caught a glimpse of the clock on the mantelpiece. Two o'clock. Dominic and Francine must have gone to bed hours ago.

Embarrassed to have fallen asleep in company, Anna decided to look for her room as quietly as possible so as not to wake them. The stairs were narrow and winding, creaking under her stockinged feet as she tiptoed up. As she reached the landing, she saw that there were two doors facing the stairs, one firmly closed, the other slightly ajar.

What made her approach that door she couldn't say, but some instinct drew her closer, yet stopped her from pushing it open. What she saw reflected in the mirror on the wall opposite made her stop in her tracks.

For a split second, she thought that Dominic was

alone. He had his back to her, though she quickly realised that she could see his face in the mirror which ran from floor to ceiling all the way along one wall.

His naked, bronzed back gleamed in the soft glow of the bedside lamps, the hard, taut contours of his buttocks drawing her gaze as she ran her eyes down the length of his body. It took a few seconds for Anna's eyes to assimilate all that she saw. It was the expression on his face that alerted her to the fact that he wasn't alone.

His eyes were closed, his expression one of total absorption. As Anna watched, a low moan forced its way through his lips and her mouth ran dry as she recognised its cause. After all, she had extracted just such a groan from him herself on many an occasion.

Pushing the door very slightly, she was not surprised to see that Dominic's hands were tangled in the dark, silky hair of the woman who was kneeling at his feet. Neither Dominic nor Francine was aware they were being watched, both were too wrapped up in what they were doing.

Anna's eyes widened as she watched the other woman's lips stretch around the bulbous head of Dominic's penis, her cheeks bulging as she took the length of him into her mouth. Jealousy, sharp and piquant, pierced her.

She should back away, before one of them saw her, yet she could not seem to make her feet move. She might be appalled by what she saw, but she was also utterly fascinated. Fascination won.

Dominic's fingers were massaging Frankie's scalp as she sucked and licked at him with relish. Anna watched, transfixed as he arched his neck back and Francine reached around and cupped his buttocks with her hands.

Her long, red-painted fingernails looked dangerous against his vulnerable skin as she squeezed and kneaded. Pressing him closer so that her face was buried in his groin, his cock slipped further into Frankie's mouth so that Anna assumed it must have reached the back of her throat.

Francine gave every appearance of enjoying fellating him. Her eyes were closed, her face glowing with pleasure. Little, mewling sounds came from her throat and her hands grasped convulsively at his buttocks as he thrust in and out of her accommodating mouth with ever increasing rhythm.

Anna was aware of a heaviness in her own sex as she watched them. She could imagine so clearly what Francine was experiencing, the sharp, salty taste of him on her tongue and the warm, rigid flesh teasing the sensitive skin of her inner cheeks. Her own sex lips swelled in empathy, a tiny pulse beating at the core of her as she sensed an almost imperceptible shift in their mood.

There was nothing leisurely about their enjoyment of each other now. Dominic's hips pumped convulsively, his face screwed up in a rictus of ecstasy. Anna could imagine Francine's powerful sucking motion on his engorged penis, could almost taste his excitement herself. They were both so beautiful, so well matched, it was a pleasure to watch them. Anna's hand strayed between her thighs and she rubbed slowly at her fabric-covered crotch.

Dominic came with a loud cry of triumph. Francine gripped him tightly as she tried valiantly to swallow the torrent of semen which gushed from him. For a few minutes they were still, Francine still holding his deflating penis in her mouth so that the only sound in the room was the harsh rasp of Dominic's breathing.

Anna continued to rub the heel of her hand rhythmically against the seam of her jeans, tantalising the swollen flesh pressing against it. When at last Dominic brought his breathing under control, he reached down and, grasping Frankie under the elbows, drew her to her feet.

Anna hadn't realised that Frankie was naked until that moment. She couldn't take her eyes from the slender perfection of the other woman's body, admiring the elegant sweep of her back and the gently rounded buttocks which were now presented to her. Her skin was a lovely honey gold, so soft and smooth that Anna itched to stroke it.

They kissed, passionately, then Dominic sank slowly to his knees, as if in homage to the woman who had brought him so much pleasure. His hands roved lovingly over the smooth skin of her thighs, lingering over the dark, coarse tangle of hair at their apex.

Anna held her breath as Francine shifted her weight slightly, parting her legs so that he, and Anna, could see the dark pink folds of flesh hidden between them. Even from her vantage point by the door, Anna could see that the tender flesh of Francine's vulva was moist. She could smell the sweet, pungent odour of feminine arousal hanging in the air of the bedroom.

Mesmerised, she watched as Dominic gently peeled back the outer lips to reveal the sensitive folds within. Running his forefinger almost reverently along the crease, he worked it in further until he found the tight little orifice which would give him access to her body.

Francine groaned as he entered her, rotating her hips so that his fingertip reached further inside her. Anna unfastened her jeans and slipped her hand inside her panties, desperate to touch herself as Dominic was touching Frankie.

It came as no surprise to her to find that she was wet. Her only problem was caging her sighs behind her teeth she stroked the moisture-slick folds of flesh, bearing down on her own finger until she made contact with the hard button which was swelling, demanding her attention.

She watched, transfixed, as, holding Francine open with his fingers, Dominic snaked out his tongue and licked along the grooves of flesh. God, she could feel his tongue pleasuring *her* sex, could empathise with every sensation Francine was experiencing.

Would she and Frankie taste very different? Anna imagined kissing Dominic after he had finished tonguing the other girl. She would be able to taste her on his lips, could experience secondhand the flavour of another woman's sex.

Appalled by the turn her thoughts had taken,

Anna rubbed herself harder, bending her knees so that she could get a second finger inside her hot, wet vagina.

Francine was approaching her climax now. Her dark hair whipped across her face and flew into Dominic's as she moved her head from side to side.

'*Alors*, Nicky, it is so good, so good! Do it to me, *mon amour*, feast on me . . .'

Anna climaxed, biting her bottom lip until she drew blood in her efforts to remain silent. Dazed, hardly able to think straight, she backed away from the doorway just as Francine began to grind her hips frantically against Dominic's face . . .

It felt cold downstairs and the sofa was lonely. Pulling the covers up, around her ears, Anna admitted to herself that she wanted nothing more than to be with the couple who were probably now enjoined on the big bed she had glimpsed in the room upstairs.

Yes, she had felt jealous when she had stumbled across them. But her jealousy was nothing compared to her desire to be a part of their love-making. What plans did Dominic have for her when he brought her here? Anna grimaced as she realised that, whatever they were, she had probably scuppered them by falling asleep!

Squeezing her thighs tightly together, she tried in vain to ease the pulse that still beat between them. She could not rid herself of the image of Francine's full red lips stretched around Dominic's cock. Behind her closed eyelids, she could still see the thick, dark hair of the other girl's mons, still glimpse the tempting, dark rose flesh nestling between her legs.

Francine was so beautiful, so fragrant. The mere sight of her soft, naked skin invited the onlooker to reach out and touch, to caress and squeeze and pleasure her . . . Restless, Anna turned her face into the back of the sofa. She didn't know what was the matter with her; she had never had these kinds of feelings for another woman before.

What would Dominic say if she told him what she had been thinking? She could find out, of course, but that would mean admitting to him that she had watched them together, and she couldn't do that. She groaned, berating herself for being no better than a peeping tom!

And yet, and yet . . . she was not altogether convinced that Dominic and Francine had been as oblivious to her presence as they had appeared. Supposing . . . no, they could not have meant for her to stumble across them like that. As far as they were concerned, she had remained fast asleep on the sofa in the living-room.

What she had seen was too personal, too private to have been meant for her eyes. Anna punched her cushion and tried to settle down. For an hour or more she tossed and turned, unable to erase the images from her mind.

For a second time, she masturbated herself to a climax, collapsing in a state of hot and sweaty exhaustion, yet still sleep eluded her. The dawn chorus had begun by the time she finally drifted off, and even then her sleep was disturbed by a series of vivid, disjointed dreams in which Frankie and Dominic always played a part.

Chapter Eight

'*DID YOU SLEEP* well, *chérie*?'

Anna sat opposite Dominic in the sunny dining-room and carefully avoided his eye as she replied.

'Yes, thank you.'

There was a small, uncomfortable silence, broken only by the clink of Francine's coffee cup against the saucer.

'You looked so peaceful, we didn't like to disturb you,' the other woman said lightly.

Her full, red lips stretched into a smile and instantly Anna was reminded of how those same lips had opened to suck in Dominic's eager cock the night before. Their eyes locked and Anna missed a breath. Frankie *knew* she had seen them, she was sure of it. But she didn't mind, if anything her eyes signalled sympathy for Anna's discomfort. The full lips moved and Anna had to force herself to concentrate on what was being said.

'The weather forecast is good today. I thought

that perhaps after breakfast you might like to go for a walk through the copse?'

'That would be lovely, don't you think, Anna?'

With two pairs of eyes turned expectantly on her, Anna nodded and attempted a smile.

Once outside in the warm, fresh air, she began to relax a little. Francine's cottage backed on to open fields which rolled down to a small copse of trees. The sun was warm on Anna's face, a light breeze caressing her skin as she walked between Francine and Dominic.

Both Dominic and Francine appeared to be relaxed and at ease after their night of passion. It clearly did not occur to Dominic that Anna might feel threatened by his relationship with the gorgeous Frenchwoman and Anna found, curiously, that she was not. In fact the most overwhelming emotion that had spilled over from the night before was the feeling of being excluded, of being left out.

Glancing at Dominic from the corner of her eye, she felt an unexpected rush of desire for him and had to fight the sudden urge to press herself against his side. As if sensing her scrutiny, he turned his head and smiled at her. Slinging a casual arm around her shoulders, he drew her against him.

The warmth of his body was reassuring and Anna realised that her greatest fear had been that what she had seen last night might have heralded the end of their liaison. Darting a furtive glance at Frankie, she was relieved that the other woman seemed totally unconcerned by Dominic's open display of affection. Frankie walked happily beside them, her dark hair caught up in a high pony tail which swung from side to side as she moved.

There was a steep incline down to the copse which slowed them down. As Anna put one foot carefully in front of the other, she slipped on a patch of wet mud and, unable to regain her balance, fell to the bottom of the slope. Landing awkwardly on her ankle she let out a muted yelp of pain.

'*Mon Dieu!* Frankie – come quickly! Anna has fallen.'

Dominic was by her side in an instant, supporting her round the shoulders, his handsome face creased with concern. Scrambling quickly down the bank, Francine homed in on the problem, cradling Anna's injured ankle gently in one slender hand.

Already the pain was beginning to subside and Anna felt foolish.

'It's all right, I just twisted it as I fell – it'll be all right in a minute . . .'

But Francine was not about to take any chances. Untying Anna's shoe laces, she peeled off her sock and examined the ankle carefully.

'I think you are right, thank God!' she remarked as she probed the tender skin gently with her fingertips. 'There is no swelling, no bruise.'

Her fingers lingered on Anna's soft, white flesh. Cradling the sore ankle with one hand, she stroked around it lightly with the fingers of her other hand, sending pleasurable little tremors feathering up Anna's leg.

Raising her eyes, she caught Anna's gaze and

smiled slowly, a lazy, knowing smile which made Anna tremble. The air around them seemed to have stilled and become muggy. That was probably why Anna suddenly found it hard to breathe; there could be no other explanation for it. The heavy, melting sensation which had started up in the pit of her stomach could only be an echo of the orgasm she had experienced the night before.

Anna shivered as she felt Dominic smooth away the heavy curtain of her hair and his lips pressed lightly against the nape of her neck. Suddenly, she was very conscious of the rich, loamy scent of the earth around them, noticing the clarity of the light as it twinkled through the thick canopy of leaves which arced above their heads.

Leaning against Dominic's chest, she sighed. Frankie smiled again before replacing Anna's sock and shoe.

'Do you think you can walk now?' she asked softly.

Anna nodded reluctantly, unwilling now to rouse herself from the sensual lethargy which had stolen over her. Dominic and Francine each took an arm and helped her to her feet. Putting her weight gingerly on the injured ankle, Anna found with some relief that she had indeed only twisted it and she was sure that it wouldn't stay sore for long. Nevertheless, she was glad when, by mutual consent, they cut their walk short and turned back towards the cottage.

'Perhaps it wasn't such a good idea to bring you down to the copse!' Frankie grimaced as they walked slowly back.

'I'm sorry – it was lovely to get some fresh air.'

'Don't worry,' Dominic said, his voice low and husky, 'I'm sure we can find plenty to fill our time . . . indoors.'

There it was again, that familiar, cramping sensation of desire streaking through her, taking her by surprise. She didn't quite know what to expect, or what was expected of her, yet somehow that unknown quantity added spice to her anticipation.

Once inside, Dominic went to make coffee while Anna and Frankie settled side by side on the sofa.

'Does it still hurt, *chérie*?'

'Not really, I just fell awkwardly, that's all. I didn't mean to make a fuss.'

'Nonsense, a twisted ankle can be very painful. Let me have another look, just to be sure.'

Anna felt curiously reluctant to have Frankie's cool hands on her skin again, but could think of no good reason why the other girl shouldn't look at her ankle. This time there was no mistaking the sensuous nature of her caresses as she stroked the skin of Anna's foot and ankle.

'Relax, *chérie*, you feel so tense,' she murmured as her fingers strayed up Anna's leg towards her calf.

The legs of Anna's jeans were too narrow to permit her to reach any higher and she was conscious of a sense of disappointment when Francine removed her hand. Easing herself on to the sofa beside her, she transferred her attention to Anna's forehead, stroking it with her fingertips and smoothing back her hair, all the while holding her gaze, her lips curving into a small smile.

'You are wary of me, no?'

'Of course not!' Anna laughed nervously.

Frankie was so close she could see the faint, fine down on the skin of her cheeks, could smell the sharp, piquant woman-scent of her as she continued to stroke her forehead. The action was strangely soothing, in counterpoint to the tension which was curling in her belly. A part of her wanted to pull away, to discourage the small intimacy, but another part of her, the greater part, wanted to stay still, to wait and see what would happen next.

She was unprepared for the sudden descent of Frankie's lips to meet hers. She gasped, unable to believe for a second that this woman was kissing her. Or that she was enjoying it.

Francine's lips were full and soft. Anna caught the scent of roses as her mouth moved over hers, coaxing her lips apart, inveigling her to open her mouth. She could feel the other woman's breasts pressing against the fullness of her own, her nipples small and pebble-hard beneath the navy rib top.

Frankie's fingertips played over her face, exploring, caressing, seeking out the most sensitive spots so that Anna's mouth opened on a sigh of pure pleasure. The intrusion of Frankie's tongue was less shocking. She tasted sweet, like Parma violets.

Pulling away slightly, Francine smiled, a slow, languorous smile which lit up her eyes. Reaching for one of Anna's hands which had lain, impotent, in her lap, she squeezed it before turning to Dominic who, Anna now saw, had

115

returned silently to the room.

'Ah, coffee! Merci, Nicky – I'm so thirsty!'

Anna raised her eyes to Dominic's nervously, sitting forward in her seat. What on earth would he make of the scene he had just come across? He was watching her, his eyes darkened with desire, though his smile was gentle.

'I knew that you and Frankie would get along,' he said softly.

Anna's eyes widened in shock and she gulped at the coffee Francine had passed to her, burning her mouth. Surely Dominic had not brought her here specifically so that Frankie could seduce her? Holding his gaze as the other girl insinuated her slender body behind her on the sofa, Anna realised that, yes, that was exactly why he had brought her to Francine's house.

The realisation sent a thrill of illicit pleasure running through her veins. Frankie sat behind her, one leg on either side of her trembling body, her bottom raised on several cushions so that when Anna responded to her suggestion that she should lean back against her, she was head and shoulders taller and Anna's head was pillowed on her small, soft breasts.

'C'est magnifique,' Dominic breathed, his eyes shining as he watched them, 'dark and light, black silk and honey gold . . .'

Anna closed her eyes for a moment as she felt Frankie's hands massaging her neck and shoulders, coaxing her to relax, to let go of her tightly bunched muscles. It was working. Anna could feel the lethargy invading her arms and legs, the warm, heavy dragging sensation of

116

burgeoning desire building low in her stomach.

She did not resist as Francine leaned over one shoulder and began to slowly unfasten the buttons of her blouse. Her breasts had swollen in their white lace restraint, the deep rose-coloured nipples hard and excited. Raising her hips, she helped Frankie remove her jeans so that in no time she was sitting on the sofa in nothing but her white lace underwear.

She could feel Frankie's tension as she leaned against her, could smell the faint, sweet perfume of her arousal as she splayed her hands across Anna's breasts.

'Take off her *brassière*, Frankie,' Dominic breathed, 'see how her skin begs you.'

Looking down at herself, Anna could see the spreading blush of colour across her chest. As Frankie pulled her bra straps down and eased the cups off her breasts, they sprang free, the nipples taut and waiting, unashamed before Dominic's hot-eyed gaze.

The other woman's hands were soft and cool as they lifted the two heavy globes of flesh, squeezing gently so that their peaks stood out in blatant invitation. Her breasts quivered as Francine let them go, bouncing gently on her rib-cage and creating an altogether different kind of tension.

Anna was past apprehension now, past caring that the hands which roamed so freely over the upper part of her body were feminine. Holding Dominic's eye, she sighed, a long, shuddering sigh. Turning her head, she sought Francine's mouth with hers, eager to taste again that distinctive, Parma violet sweetness.

Frankie's hair fell like a fragrant curtain over the two of them, shielding Anna's face and muffling her muted groans.

'You are so beautiful, my darling,' Francine breathed, rubbing her cheek, catlike, against Anna's before kissing her again.

Anna whimpered, deep in her throat, as Dominic knelt at her feet and peeled away her damp panties. She could smell her own arousal rising from her slippery sex.

Dominic returned to his chair, taking her panties with him as he watched them. Anna gasped as Frankie's long, cool fingers played teasingly around the edge of her mons. Unable to help herself, she shifted her bottom, allowing her thighs to fall apart.

'*Enchanté*,' Dominic whispered. 'See how wet she is, Francine, feel her heat.'

'All in good time, *mon amour*,' Frankie admonished gently. 'This is Anna's first time with another woman, we must not rush her.'

Anna bit down on her lower lip lest the shaming denial should escape through them. Heaven help her, she wanted nothing more than to feel Francine's small, female hands cupping her sex, peeling back her labia to expose the glistening inner flesh to Dominic's gaze.

Even without being touched she was so close to the edge of orgasm she felt as though she would come the minute Frankie went near her. But Francine was clever. Perhaps it was because she was a woman, she knew exactly how to prolong the pleasure. Anna moaned softly as her inner thighs were massaged rhythmically, the expert movement pulling on the tender skin of her vulva, sending indirect messages of delight to her innermost flesh.

Dominic was breathing more slowly now, each outward breath coming in a long sigh.

'Touch her, *chérie* – you want her to touch you, Anna, no?'

'No . . . oh yes, please yes!'

Francine's warm, wicked chuckle vibrated against her back as her fingers lingered on her thighs, brushing gently over the golden curls which shielded her most sensitive skin. Anna held her breath, watching Dominic's hands close over the tumescence at the front of his trousers through half closed eyes.

When at last Frankie ran the tip of one fingernail along the groove of her sex and up the other side, it was all Anna could do not to cry out. The light, teasing touch was unbearable, sending her quickly to a screaming pitch of frustration.

'Please, oh please!'

Her head thrashed from side to side as she begged the other girl to grant her the release which was so close, and yet just beyond her reach.

Francine kissed her deeply as her fingers unerringly found the hard nub of flesh which was yearning for her touch. Anna thrust her hips forward to meet her hand, opening her legs wider to stretch the skin and so derive the greatest pleasure. Dominic's voice, vibrating with passion, seemed to come from far away.

'That's it, *chérie*, make her come . . . see how her sex streams, how she loves it! Make her ready for me . . .'

The combination of Dominic's explicit words and Frankie's knowing touch tipped Anna over the edge. Her thigh muscles jerked as she came, her entire body focussed on that small spot of pleasure which Frankie had stimulated beyond the point of no return.

Reaching her arms up, behind her head, she drew Frankie's head down to hers, raining tiny, grateful kisses all over her face as she sobbed her thanks.

When, at last, the tumult of sensation had died down, Anna turned her head to find Dominic had stripped naked and was kneeling between her knees. His strong, engorged penis was poised at the entrance to her body.

He seemed to be waiting for her to acknowledge him, to invite him in. Francine reached down to place the palms of her hands on Anna's inner thighs. She held Anna's legs apart, presenting her upturned sex to Dominic, positioning her for his convenience.

Anna's arms left Francine's neck and reached for Dominic as, holding her eye, he sank slowly into her. The angle of her body gave him the greatest possible penetration and Anna gasped at the slight discomfort when he reached the neck of her womb.

'Ssh,' he soothed her, his fingers caressing the sensitive hollows of her neck and running lightly over her breasts.

Leaning forward, his mouth found hers, his hard lips an exciting contrast to Frankie's soft kisses. Tears sprang to Anna's eyes as he moved slowly in and out of her and he stopped.

'Am I hurting you, *chérie?*' he asked softly.

Anna shook her head and smiled through her tears, unable to put into words the strength of emotion she was experiencing. At that moment she felt such love for the two people pleasuring her she was incoherent with it.

She did not need to speak. The look in Dominic's eyes told her clearly that he understood exactly how she felt. He had never looked at her before with quite so much love in his eyes and the emotion added a finer, deeper dimension to their love-making.

Drawing him to her, Anna urged him to resume his thrusting into her. Francine curved her body around Anna's back and rode with them to the peak of pleasure. As the first seed began to pump from Dominic's body, Frankie cupped Anna's chin and turned her head so that she could kiss her.

This time, Anna kissed her back, returning her passion in equal measure as her womb contracted in sympathy with Dominic and their three heads leaned together, mouths, foreheads, cheeks all touching in one shared ascent to that other plane where physical sensation is all.

Chapter Nine

IT WAS SEVERAL minutes before any of them moved. When they did, Francine climbed stiffly from the sofa and disappeared through the door. Anna stared at Dominic wordlessly.

Dominic kissed her with a tenderness which brought fresh tears to her eyes. Seeing them glittering on her lashes, he wiped them away with his thumbpad, his eyes scanning hers.

'It's all right,' he whispered, 'it's all right.'

Anna nodded, attempting a watery smile. Dominic returned it, clearly satisfied by her response.

'Come – Frankie is running the shower. You would like to shower, no?'

Anna could think of nothing she would like better and she gratefully grasped the hand that Dominic held out to her. Still naked, they wandered up the stairs together.

Francine was already luxuriating under the warm spray and it was a few minutes before she made way for Anna. Through the steamy shower glass, she could see Frankie and Dominic embrace and break apart before Frankie left the room. She smiled as Dominic joined her.

It was blissful to merely stand under the cascade of warm water and allow someone else to soap her. Dominic worked up a creamy lather all over her body, lingering over her breasts and her now sleeping sex, working his soapy hands thoroughly into her bottom cleft.

Anna clenched her buttocks as his fingers brushed against the forbidden entrance to her body, instinctively repelled by such an intimacy. Feeling his lips curve into a smile against the slippery skin of her shoulder, she arched her neck, encouraging him to nuzzle the sensitive area behind her ear.

Incredibly, she felt the stirrings of desire re-kindle as his lips roved lightly down her neck and his soapy hands cupped her wet breasts. She moaned in protest as Dominic reluctantly let her go.

'Frankie will be waiting for us,' he explained with an apologetic grimace. 'We mustn't neglect her any more.'

Remembering Francine's unselfish giving of pleasure, Anna realised that the other girl had received no satisfaction in return. She must be simmering with passion by now and Anna felt a dart of sympathy for her. Dominic was right, they mustn't linger selfishly in the shower. Not this time.

Frankie had dressed and had set the coffee table with dainty sandwiches and bite-sized cakes. Anna hadn't realised until then how hungry she was.

'Oh Frankie, you've done nothing but feed us all weekend!' she exclaimed as she helped herself to a sandwich.

'*Nothing, chérie*?' Francine replied with a slight lift of one perfeclty shaped eyebrow.

Anna blushed furiously and Frankie smiled. With a quick glance at Anna, Dominic went to sit next to Francine, placing his arm around her shoulder and kissing her on the cheek.

'You've been very patient, *chérie*. Perhaps after we've eaten we'll all be feeling more ... energetic?'

They all laughed, though Anna had the feeling that Dominic had only been half joking. She was quite relieved when Frankie suggested a trip into town after lunch.

Dominic insisted that they eat out after touring the local cathedral and walking along the river bank. Giving in gracefully, Frankie directed them to a small Indian restaurant specialising in Balti dishes.

It was late when finally they half fell, laughing, through Francine's front door.

'Such fun, and the food was good too, wasn't it?'

Anna nodded, linking her arm through Francine's as they began, by unspoken mutual consent, to climb the stairs. They turned in unison as Dominic cleared his throat loudly.

'Haven't you forgotten someone?' he asked, his smile ironic as he lounged against the end of the bannister rail.

He looked so appealing with his dark hair unruly over his forehead, his expression a mixture of amusement and little-boy bewilderment. Anna and Francine looked at each other and burst out laughing.

'*Merde*, Nicky, you are a big boy now! Can't you bear the thought of sleeping alone for just one night?'

Anna sobered as the meaning of Francine's words sank in. Was the other girl assuming that, after her capitulation in the living-room this afternoon, she would be willing to actually sleep with her? She couldn't deny that she had enjoyed her unexpected Sapphic initiation, nor would she want to. But it was all so new to her, so recent and she hadn't had time to analyse how she felt about it.

Sensing her withdrawal, Frankie turned her beautiful eyes on her.

'What do you think, *chérie*?' she asked lightly, 'shall we allow him to join us?'

'Yes!' Anna replied with alacrity, biting her lip as Francine lifted one perfectly plucked eyebrow expressively. 'I mean . . . it would be nice,' she added with a grin.

Frankie touched the back of her hand against Anna's, whether in reassurance or desire, Anna could not tell. Bounding up the stairs two at a time, Dominic smiled warmly at them both as he reached them.

'You weren't really going to leave me out, were you, Frankie?' he asked, though Anna could tell from the expression on his face that he would never have allowed such a thing.

Frankie clearly realised it too for she raised herself up on her tiptoes to kiss his cheek, saying, with a sparkle of mischief in her eyes, 'But of course, *mon amour*!'

She squealed as Dominic slapped her playfully on the bottom and they all walked into the bedroom together.

To hide her sudden trepidation from the others, Anna walked over to the window and looked out. Through the darkness she could make out the shape of the trees in the garden as they swayed in the light summer breeze. The window was open and she could smell the scent of the flowers lingering in the air, combining with that fresh, crisp scent that perfumes the evening air after a long, hot day in summer.

Turning, she saw that the room was dominated by a large, white lace covered bed which was piled high with cushions and pillows at one end. Removing his shoes and socks and his jacket, Dominic made himself comfortable at the bed head.

Smiling at Anna, he produced an ice bucket from the bedside cabinet and three glasses.

'Remembering how you like champagne, I put some on ice before we left.'

Anna smiled, feeling sick with nerves, her eyes skittering to the dainty little dressing table in the corner where Francine was brushing her hair. Their eyes met in the mirror and Anna quickly looked away.

She couldn't do this, she thought frantically as she turned back to the window. Earlier, things had happened so spontaneously she hadn't had time to think, or worry. Now their coming up the stairs together like this seemed so cold-blooded, so clinical . . . she jumped as she felt Frankie's cool fingers brush against her cheek.

'Relax, *chérie,* there is nothing to be afraid of,' she murmured huskily.

Anna closed her eyes and swallowed as quiet, gentle music began to play, curling round her senses and soothing her. Frankie picked the pins from her hair and let them fall soundlessly to the carpet as she combed out the heavy tresses with her fingers. Then she began to brush Anna's hair with long, firm strokes which made her scalp tingle.

Staring fixedly out into the darkened garden, Anna allowed herself to succumb slowly to the inevitability of it all. Having her hair brushed like this was curiously soothing, a experience which was sensual in a way that she would never have thought possible.

Her eyes felt heavy-lidded, her limbs melting slowly into the heat of desire as Francine rubbed her cheek against the now silken fall of Anna's hair. Reaching round her, she pulled the curtains across the window, enclosing them, wrapping them into their own confined world where the usual mores and tenets of Anna's life had no place.

Uttering a long, low sign of surrender, Anna turned round slowly. Francine's eyes widened in surprise as the initiative was taken from her and Anna drew her close. The hairbrush dropped to the floor with a muted thump as it slipped through her fingers.

Little thrills of excitement chased each other through Anna's body as she moved her lips over

Frankie's. The other girl felt soft and compliant in her arms, her weight slight as she leaned against her. A surge of assertiveness, more powerful than any aphrodisiac, took Anna by surprise. Lifting her mouth from Frankie's, she looked over to the bed where her gaze collided with Dominic's.

Her breath caught in her throat at the look he gave her. Holding her eye over the rim of his glass, he sipped at his champagne. Unsmiling, eyes signalling his lambent desire, Anna picked up on his tension and was herself affected by it. Without at first realising what she was doing, she tightened her grip on Frankie's waist, pulling her body tighter against hers.

Dominic remained silent, though his eyes urged her on, filling her with a new feeling. Pride made her hold his eye as she ran her hands lovingly down Frankie's sides and back up again. Suddenly she wanted nothing more than to prove to Dominic how far she had come since they had met.

Francine whimpered deep in her throat as Anna cupped one breast in her palm. She was wearing a soft cotton dress in red which moulded the perfection of her form, untrammelled by any visible underwear lines. Anna felt a short, sharp stab of desire in her stomach as the nipple hardened and swelled under her hand.

For her own sake, now, she wanted nothing more than to feel Francine's naked skin grow warm at her touch. Before, she had lain passive in the other girl's arms whilst her own latent senses were awakened. This time, she wanted more, so much more. To touch, to taste, to explore

Francine's body as she had Dominic's. To possess her.

Anna was barely aware of the music which soared and climaxed around them before starting again. Her attention was focussed entirely on undressing the girl now standing compliantly in front of her, a small, catlike smile of anticipation curving her lips upward.

'I want to see you naked.'

Her own voice was alien to her as she whispered the words. To her amazement and pleasure, Francine immediately curled her fingers around the hem of her dress and pulled it up, over her head before casting it aside. As Anna had suspected, Frankie was completely naked underneath.

Her mouth and throat felt dry as she gazed at her. The honey-gold of her skin was lent a pearlised sheen by the soft glow of the lamps placed either side of her bed. Her small breasts were crested by two nut-brown buttons of flesh which strained towards Anna, inviting her to touch.

Suddenly, Anna was at a loss, feeling some of her confidence ebb swiftly away as she was awed by the enormity of what she was about to do. Her eyes must have given away her panic, for Francine smiled and reached for Anna's own dress buttons, helping her out of her clothes so that she too stood naked at the foot of the bed.

Anna heard Dominic's sharp intake of breath, but did not take her eyes off Francine. She wanted so much to snatch back the initiative for herself, to bend the beautiful woman standing inches

129

away from her to her will, extracting every ounce of pleasure from her as Francine had from her earlier.

Tentatively, she reached out a hand to touch Francine's cheek. Her skin was soft and unblemished, slightly moist beneath her fingers. Tracing a path around the oval of her face, up, along her hairline and down to her gently rounded chin, Anna admired every feature. The unusual, slightly slanted eyes were framed, she saw now, by a double row of sooty black eyelashes.

Her nose was small, but straight, her mouth wide and generous, the lips naturally red and soft. Falling like a glossy black curtain across her narrow shoulders, her hair parted simply in the middle, framing her face in black silk.

As Anna ran the tip of one finger along the line of her lips, Francine darted out her tongue and licked it. Anna jumped, but did not remove her hand. Instead she watched, mesmerised as Frankie drew in the tip of her finger and sucked on it.

An answering pull tugged deep in her womb and Anna held her breath, letting it out on a sigh as Frankie turned her face into her hand and licked the centre of her palm. All hesitation gone now, Anna pulled Francine urgently into her arms, revelling in the sensation of skin on skin as their lips fused in another kiss.

Frankie's tongue was rough as it played and parried with Anna's. A vision of what Dominic could see pushed itself into her mind, sending a fresh rush of moisture to her sex. The scent of feminine arousal lay heavily in the air, a sweet, musky perfume which Anna had never dreamt could arouse her.

They were both panting slightly as they broke apart and Anna was sure the flush in Francine's cheeks would be in hers too. Chancing a glance at Dominic, she saw he was watching them through heavy-lidded eyes, though he made no attempt to join them.

Wordlessly, he passed them both a glass and leaned forward to fill them with champagne. Anna gulped at hers greedily, welcoming the lubrication to her throat and mouth. Frankie barely touched hers, raising it to her lips briefly before abandoning it on the bedside table. Climbing on to the bed, she allowed her hair to fall across her shoulders, sweeping over Dominic's legs.

Anna could not take her eyes off the small, rounded globes of her breasts hanging down from her rib-cage as she remained on all fours. Her pert bottom was out-thrust, giving Dominic a perfect view of her open sex.

Kneeling up slowly, she held out her arms to Anna. Needing no further invitation, Anna was galvanised into action. Kneeling opposite Frankie on the bed, inches away from Dominic, she took the other woman into her arms.

Their nipples kissed, foreheads pressed together, lips and tongues entwining. Francine's skin was like warm silk beneath her palms as Anna ran her hands down her back and up her arms, stroking her shoulders. A pulse fluttered at the base of the other girl's neck and Anna pressed her lips against it, urging her to lie back on the bed, across Dominic's feet.

Now she had her lying prone in front of her, Anna's gaze roved her still body, hardly knowing where to begin. Her eyes moved towards Dominic as he spoke.

'Feel how soft is her skin, *chérie*, here—' he touched his fingertips briefly to the base of Francine's neck, 'and here,' he ran his fingers in a light caress along the inside of her upper arm.

Anna leaned forward and touched her lips against the areas he had indicated, breathing in the warm, musky scent of Frankie's skin, allowing it to intoxicate her. Dominic's voice was murmurous in her ear as he urged her to touch and taste, to abandon all inhibition.

Francine lay compliant, watching Anna, silent save for the soft moans and sighs which occasionally escaped through her parted lips.

'Suck her nipples, Anna, roll them on your tongue.'

Anna complied, playing with one brown crest while she licked and nibbled gently on the other. She had always wondered how Dominic must feel when they were making love; now she could feel and taste a woman's body for herself. Though the man on the bed with them was watching her every move, she did not feel directed by him, glad as she was for his quietly spoken suggestions.

He stroked her hair as she left Frankie's breasts and licked at the salty droplets of sweat pooling between them. Raising herself up, her eyes roved greedily over the other woman's body, drinking in the harmonious shape of her breasts and hips as they flared gently from the narrow waist.

'Turn over,' she whispered huskily.

Francine shivered, her skin rising up in goosebumps as Anna ran her forefinger down the length of her spine to her coccyx. Lingering over the tender dimple at its base, she admired the smoothness of the other girl's skin, envying its flawless, honey-gold perfection.

The soft light of the lamps illuminated the fine down in the small of her back and Anna stroked it lightly with her fingertips, watching as it stood on end to meet her touch. Between her thighs, the deep dark well of her secret flesh tempted her, drew her fingers and her lips as she kissed a path down the length of her spine.

She could smell the sweet, fruity scent of feminine arousal. The other girl shuddered as Anna moulded the shape of her buttocks with both hands and gently parted her bottom cheeks. That forbidden nether mouth seemed to shrink from the shame of exposure and, acting on impulse, Anna circled it lightly with her finger, fascinated to see the spincter of muscle contract convulsively.

'See the effect you are having on her?'

Dominic's tongue outlined the shape of Anna's outer ear as she turned her attention to the tempting flesh which lay beneath Frankie's bottom cleft. The intimate feminine flesh was swollen and red under the protective cover of the soft pubic hair.

Gently, Anna parted her sex lips with her thumbs to expose the soft, wet opening within.

Her thumbpads sank into the warm flesh as easily as if they were sinking into a ripe peach. Clear, slippery moisture coated her thumbs.

'Is she warm, *chérie*? Does she open for you?'

Anna murmured incoherent assent. 'Oh yes,' she breathed, 'oh ye-es!'

As she spoke her fingers instinctively stroked along the moisture-slick grooves of flesh either side of Frankie's inner labia, easing her path and coaxing the hot, soft flesh to open. Francine wriggled her bottom slightly, pressing her pelvis into Dominic's legs so that her vulva was displayed more clearly.

Anna smiled as she realised what the girl was trying to do. Her clitoris had come into view now, a red, swollen bud which begged to be touched. Teasing, she circled it lightly, slipping one hand underneath the girl's body so that she could massage her mons with the heel of her hand, thus applying indirect pressure to that central point of pleasure.

Francine moaned, deep in her throat. Knowing how deliciously frustrating the caress would be, Anna prolonged it until she could resist no longer and her fingers crept back towards the most sensitive flesh. Frankie's sex had opened now like a flower in the sun. Fascinated by the intricate shape of this most feminine of places, Anna took her time to stroke and explore.

That her touch should cause a fresh seepage of juices from the other girl's body gave Anna a thrill unlike anything she had ever experienced before. It was like making love to herself, so closely did Frankie's sighs and squirmings mirror her own reactions. As familiar as she was with the female body, she knew just when to apply more pressure and when to hold back, when to stroke gently along the folds and when to rub harder.

Vaguely, Anna was aware of Dominic massaging her neck and shoulders, his palm on the nape of her neck urging her to dip her head. In the back of her mind, she knew what it was he wanted her to do, but a part of her rebelled, made him wait until *she* was ready to comply.

Frankie's hair lay in damp strands on her forehead as she moved her head from side to side, almost as if delirious.

'Ahh, it is so good, Ann-a, so good . . . please . . . oh, don't stop,' she pleaded, her voice breathy, 'please don't stop!'

Anna had no intention of stopping, not now. Reaching for the pillows arranged around Dominic, she eased one underneath Francine's stomach so that it was supporting her, raising her up. Anna's tongue licked nervously along her lips, tasting salt on her upper lip. Now that she was aware of it, she realised her whole body was hot, and tense with anticipation.

Slowly, so slowly that Francine and Dominic both seemed to hold their breath as one, Anna lowered her head and buried her face in the moist, fragrant folds of Francine's sex. She tasted unexpectedly sweet, her feminine juices coating Anna's tongue like warm honey. It seemed natural to trace the grooves on either side of her labia with the tip of her tongue, circling the hard button of her clitoris before pressing the flatter part of her tongue against it.

It quivered enticingly against her tongue and Anna guessed that Francine was very close to coming. She didn't want that, not just yet. Raising her head, she peeled back the folds of flesh and gazed in fascination at the many layers of aroused flesh.

Pressing her thumbs slightly into the soft, pulpy hole of her vagina, she held it open so that she could see the dark rose, ribbed flesh of that inner tube. Gently, she inserted the whole of her forefinger, delighting in the way Francine's vaginal muscles sucked in the tentative digit, closing around it lovingly.

So this was how a man's penis must feel as it enters a woman's body. Enclosed, protected, *loved* . . .

Withdrawing her finger slowly, she smeared the thick moisture up and along Frankie's bottom cleft, lubricating the tight, puckered opening which fluttered convulsively under her gaze. On an impulse, Anna dipped her head and licked firmly from the rim of her vagina up to her anus.

The skin tasted sharper here, less sweet, more piquant. Flicking her tongue from anus to vagina and back again was like sampling a peculiar sweet and sour speciality. She would have liked to have lingered longer, but Frankie's moans were becoming more desperate now and she felt she had to give her the release for which she had already waited for so long.

She was so wet now her moisture smeared across Anna's lips as she licked a path back to the frantically pulsating clitoris. So swollen was it by now that it almost seemed to rear up and meet her questing tongue. Knowing instinctively what would bring the most pleasure, Anna flicked her tongue rapidly back and forth over the rigid flesh until the first beat of orgasm began to pulse through the small bud.

It was then that she pressed her tongue firmly against the bud, remaining stoically in place as Francine gave out a wild, animal cry and began to grind her bottom back against Anna's face. As the unmistakeable, heavy pulsing came, Anna lashed her clitoris with her tongue before drawing it between her lips and sucking on it, hard, drawing out every ounce of feeling until Francine began to cry out and beg for her to stop.

Feeling the spent button of flesh lying acquiescent now against her tongue, Anna reluctantly let it go. Raising her head, her eyes glowing with triumph, her gaze clashed with Dominic's and she grinned.

His eyes signalled his pride in her as he rose and took off the rest of his clothes. When he was naked, he leaned forward and, catching Anna's face between his palms, he kissed her hard on the mouth. She melted against him, exhausted by her efforts, unresisting as he eased her back against the pillows and bent her legs at the knees. Happy for him to arrange her for his pleasure, she felt the soft kiss of the cool evening air on her most hidden places as he parted her knees.

Frankie was sitting up now and her eyes feasted on the sight of Anna thus displayed as licentiously as did Dominic. Anna felt her inner flesh tingle and swell in response to their regard, fresh moisture gathering at the lip of her vagina and spilling over to run in a viscous trickle down her perineum and along her bottom cleft.

After a few minutes, Dominic and Frankie looked at each other, a look so laden with meaning that Anna felt her stomach knot with tension. It wasn't until Francine shifted position so that she was kneeling between Anna's thighs that Anna realised what they intended.

Dominic's cock was rigid, its circumcised tip oozing a drop of pre-emission as he stood behind Frankie. Anna's tongue snaked between her lips as she longed to take it in her mouth. It was useless to waste her longings, though; she knew that Dominic's beautiful cock was not meant for her tonight. At least, not yet.

She shuddered at the first touch of Frankie's tongue against the sensitive skin of her perineum, though she didn't take her eyes from Dominic's. He was watching her closely, gauging her every reaction, enjoying her enjoyment.

Excitement cramped in her belly as she watched him position himself behind Frankie's upraised rump. Without breaking eye contact with Anna, he eased himself into her hot, wet body, a shuddering sigh of bliss escaping through his lips.

'Oh Anna, if you could only feel what I feel now!' he whispered urgently. 'She is so hot, so tight . . .'

Anna groaned as Frankie's tongue moved in concert with Dominic's silkily seductive words. Humiliation washed over her as she realised how easily they were manipulating her sexual response. And yet she knew, even through the fog of her arousal, that the shame she felt was yet another gift.

'Is she not beautiful, *chérie*?' Dominic asked her, tangling his fingers in the dark silk of Francine's hair and tugging gently to persuade her to raise her head.

She gazed at Anna through eyes that were glassy with lust. Her lips and chin shone with Anna's juices and as she watched, she poked out her tongue and licked at them with something approaching relish. It was an act so lewd, so inherently indecent, that Anna could feel the first tingling of orgasm.

Her mouth and throat ran dry as she watched Frankie, her slight body buffeted by the increasing rhythm of Dominic's thrusting. Suddenly, she threw back her head and cried out, just as Dominic gave a strangled cry and clutched her hips tightly against his body.

Witnessing their mutual orgasm made Anna come, even though no one was touching her. With a whimper of release, she sat up and wrapped her arms around Frankie, her fingers coming up against the hot, solid wall of Dominic's chest. As one, they collapsed, Anna on to her back, Francine on top of her, Dominic still buried in her body.

They lay, a mess of limbs and combining sweat and sexual fluids, all fighting for breath, for recovery, until, at last, Anna began to feel the weight of them pressing on top of her and she shifted restlessly.

Rolling off Francine, Dominic gathered Anna's limp body against him, raining kisses on her face and neck as he murmured words of love and admiration in her ear. Meanwhile, Frankie moulded herself around Anna's body and fell immediately asleep, her head on Anna's shoulder.

Anna lay looking up into the darkness, listening to Francine's deep, even breathing for what seemed like a long time. Dominic stroked her hair, her breasts, the swell of her belly and down her thighs, soothing her, gentling her, until at last her pulse rate returned to normal.

She could not remember a time when she had felt so happy, so *complete*. Hugging this feeling to her, at last she slept.

Chapter Ten

LEAVING THE FOLLOWING morning was a wrench.

'Do you have to go, Nicky? Can't you both stay here until you go home on Sunday?'

Dominic pulled Francine close and kissed the top of her head.

'I wish we could, *chérie*, but I promised Alan I would not miss the lecture this afternoon. You will be coming to stay soon though, won't you?'

Frankie pouted prettily though she sounded philosophical.

'Yes, very soon. What about Anna though? Are you going to come to the château with me?'

Anna blushed as both pairs of eyes turned on her expectantly. Conscious that it wasn't Dominic who had asked her she could hardly interpret Frankie's words as an invitation. Yet Dominic appeared to be waiting for her reply as eagerly as was Francine.

'Well, I . . . you're forgetting my husband, Frankie!' she laughed.

Frankie snorted.

'*Mais non, ma chère*, it is *you* who should be forgetting this husband of yours!'

Dominic put his arm around Anna.

'You over-step the mark, Francine,' he said quietly.

'No, please,' Anna jumped in hastily, 'I'm not offended, Dominic. I . . . I suppose I haven't had time to think about what I'm going to do about Paul yet . . .' she trailed off, biting her lip uncertainly.

'Only you can decide, Anna. But you will always be welcome at my home if that is what you decide you want.'

Anna felt her cheeks grow warm with pleasure as she realised the great compliment that Dominic was paying her. Francine smiled encouragingly at her.

'Dominic is right, I should not have said what I did. But whatever happens, Anna, you and I will always be friends, no?'

Anna stepped forward and kissed the girl on the cheek.

'Always,' she whispered fervently.

She was silent for most of the journey home. Dominic's invitation had surprised and thrilled her. More than that, it had made her realise that there were other avenues open to her other than trying to save her seriously flagging marriage. Nor was it an either-or situation. She could simply decide to go it alone.

From feeling there was only one way forward to realising the whole plethora of opportunities open to her was a giant mental step. It was no wonder she was feeling dizzy!

Once home Anna made them both lunch before Dominic left for the college. Quashing a pang of guilt for staying at home sick when she was nothing of the sort, she began to tidy the house. Somehow, though, the familiar routine of housework irritated rather than soothed her and so she dispensed with the essentials as quickly as possible, cutting corners shamelessly.

At four o'clock, she took herself upstairs and ran herself a bath. It felt deliciously decadent to be sinking into a tub full of fragrant bubbles in the middle of the afternoon. Lying back, she closed her eyes and imagined Dominic lecturing in the auditorium.

Would he spare a thought for her as he held forth, or would the captivated gaze of a dozen female students distract him? She smiled as she soaped her body. It didn't matter what he might be doing now, the fact was in a couple of hours he was coming home to *her*.

The past week had been like a period out of time, an almost surreal experience which had nothing to do with her normal life. Would she revert back to her old self when Dominic went back to France on Sunday?

She frowned as she thought of how imminent was his departure. Whatever happened, she knew she would cherish this short time she had spent with him. She had learned far more about herself and her own sexuality in one short week with Dominic than she had in five years of marriage to Paul.

Indulging herself, she lay back in the bath and

closed her eyes again. The warm water lapped gently around her body, enclosing her in an almost womblike state which was curiously comforting. Allowing her mind to wander free, Anna thought of her most recent experiences with Francine, and smiled.

With hindsight, she knew she had 'clicked' with Frankie from that first night when they had watched the woman called Fleuris perform on stage at that strange club. To think that Frankie had climaxed at the same time as she had, courtesy of the same man, and she hadn't even realised . . .

Her mind turned back to Fleuris. She had thought at the time how wonderfully she had danced. Remembering how she had promised herself that she would dance like that for Dominic one day, Anna smiled. She would surprise him tonight when he came home.

Now that the idea had taken hold, Anna couldn't wait to set her plans in motion. Leaving the bath, she wrapped herself in a towel and went through to her bedroom. Once dry, she dropped the towel and scrutinised her appearance in the mirror doors of her wardrobes.

She smiled as she recalled that a mere week ago she had done the same thing, yet oh so surreptitiously, as if she was doing something inherently *wrong* by looking at her own body! She laughed aloud as she realised how much more confident she was now. Dominic's love-making had liberated her in a way she would never have thought possible.

It might be her imagination, but she was sure

that she even *looked* different now. Her skin glowed with health, her eyes harbouring a sparkle which had been missing before. She looked, she admitted to herself with a small thrill of satisfaction, like a woman who was fulfilled, in every sense of the word.

Letting her hair fall free around her shoulders, she marvelled that she should ever have believed herself to be plain. The woman smiling seductively back at her in the mirror was beautiful, sure of her own sensual power in a way that the timid girl who had stood in this same spot a few days ago had never hoped to be.

She didn't need music to dance, she could hear it in her head. Moving her hips from side to side, she shook her head so that her long, silky hair brushed over her breasts, tickling her nipples. The gentle stimulation encouraged them to grow rosy and hard and she lifted her breasts with her hands, pinching the crests between thumb and forefinger.

Bearing in mind what would delight Dominic most, she gyrated and swayed, one eye always on the mirror so that she could gauge how best to present herself. After half an hour she collapsed, pink and perspiring, on to the bed. It hadn't looked this much like hard work when Fleuris had danced!

Raising her arms up above her head, she imagined Dominic's pleasure and his subsequent expression of it. The mere thought of him taking her into his arms sent desire cramping through her stomach and she rose quickly, steadfastly ignoring it. Saving herself for him.

145

Rummaging through her drawers, she came across the suspender set her sister Leigh had bought her before her wedding.

'I've never met a man who *wasn't* a sucker for black stockings and suspenders,' she had said.

Anna had soon found out that Paul was the exception to this rule. Her face clouded as she remembered how, when she had tried to tempt him with Leigh's gift, he had called her a tart and a whore.

Well, she told herself as she caressed the cobweb fine lace with her fingertips, Dominic wouldn't mind if she played the whore whilst she was with him!

The suspender belt fitted snugly round her waist, the suspenders forming a stark frame for the golden curls on her pubis. As part of her gift, Leigh had wrapped three pairs of sheer black stockings. There were still two unopened packets at the back of her drawer and Anna brought one of these out now. The stockings rolled on easily, coating her legs in luxuriously fine Lycra which fastened to the suspenders.

On an impulse she left the matching panties at the back of the drawer, imagining Dominic's delight at discovering what she had done. Her breasts had to be persuaded into the heavily wired, black 'uplift' bra which had remained unworn at the back of her underwear drawer for years. She had never quite been able to bring herself to get rid of it and looking at her reflection she thought she knew why.

Her breasts overflowed over the top of the lacy cups, two creamy globes of flesh whose sheer abundance was a temptation to behold. Maybe she had never quite given up on her own sexuality, she acknowledged silently. Hope was a sexy black bra stuffed at the back of a drawer.

Pushing her feet into her highest stiletto heels, she covered up the sight of her lasciviously displayed body with the nondescript, safe black shift which she had worn on most social occasions she had attended with Paul. Piling her hair up on her head in a loose topknot, she applied her make-up before going downstairs, hugging her secret to her with almost childlike glee.

Dominic grinned at her when he walked in at six-thirty.

'Did you think I was never coming back, *chérie*?' he asked her playfully as she stood up to greet him.

'I would have been very surprised,' she replied, walking confidently into his arms and drawing him to her with his tie.

If he was surprised by the passion of her kiss he didn't show it, putting his arms around her shoulders and pressing her to him. Just as she felt his arousal grow, Anna pulled away.

'I thought we'd go out to eat tonight,' she told him, hiding a smile at the quick expression of dismay in his eyes which he wasn't quick enough to conceal. Clearly he had other ideas about where he wanted to spend his evening.

He was too much of a gentleman to protest, though, and took the shortest possible time to freshen up and change. Within the hour they were sitting at the table she had reserved earlier at a small Italian bistro not far from the house.

Throughout the meal of fresh pasta and creamy

ham and mushroom sauce, Anna played footsie with Dominic under the table, aware from the look in his eyes that she was succeeding in her aim to keep him on the edge of arousal. His pupils were dilated and he kept giving her half puzzled, half intrigued glances as if he could not quite fathom her mood.

Anna revelled in the rush of power she felt at being in control. Constantly aware of her semi-nakedness beneath the outwardly respectable dress, she longed to tell him, to see his face as he realised. Moistening her throat with the crisp white wine, she slipped off one of her shoes and, under the cover of the cheerful gingham-checked table cloth, she rested her foot carefully between his legs.

He half choked on his wine as her toes played with his erection, but his eyes were amused rather than censorious and Anna was encouraged to continue. It was uncomfortable though, trying to stimulate him within the confines of the table and her calf muscles soon began to protest. So with a small sigh of regret, she let her foot slide slowly back down the inside of his leg.

She waited until they were eating the smooth chocolate mousse they were served for sweet before leaning forward and whispering, 'I'm not wearing any knickers.'

She watched his face closely as he failed to conceal either his initial shock, or the faint blush of arousal which crept under his skin.

'Let's go back,' he said hoarsely as soon as he had recovered.

Anna smiled slowly. 'I'd like some coffee first –

wouldn't you?' she asked innocently, catching the eye of their waiter.

Dominic waited until the young man had left before saying under his breath, 'You are playing the tease tonight, Anna?'

She smiled and raised an eyebrow. Dominic caught hold of her hand and turned it, palm upwards, so that her knuckles rested on the table. Lightly tracing the lines on the surface of her skin with his fingertip, he held her gaze as he murmured, 'Be careful, *chérie* – you are playing with fire. Could it be that you are *hoping* to get burnt?'

Anna welcomed the tight knot of tension which coiled in her belly as he smiled at her. Her hand balled into a fist involuntarily, grasping his finger as he pressed its tip against the very centre of her palm.

The arrival of the waiter with their coffee broke the tension. Anna sipped at the thick, black liquid without really tasting it, her eyes never leaving Dominic's. They burned like coals, boring into her so that she fancied he could see right through her pretence of respectability to the licentious whore beneath.

A dull pulse throbbed between her legs as she imagined his reaction when she removed her clothes and he saw what she had been wearing underneath. Now it was she who could not wait to leave.

They walked home in silence, oblivious to the starry beauty of the evening. Once inside, Dominic would have drawn her in his arms in the hallway and taken her there, on the Axminster, but Anna was determined to remain in control, at least for now. Slipping out of his grasp, she sashayed through to the living-room, throwing him what she hoped was a 'come hither' look over her shoulder as she reached the door.

He raised a quizzical eyebrow at her as she poured him a generous measure of brandy and pushed him firmly down on to the sofa. Having gone to great lengths to set things up before he arrived home from the college, it took her mere minutes to switch on the lamps she had placed strategically round the room.

A funky medley was all ready on the CD player, set to continuous play so that she wouldn't be taken unawares by the music ending too soon. Nerves fluttered through her as she switched it on and took up the position she had decided was best on the floor in front of him. He was watching her every move through heavy-lidded eyes, his tension palpable in the air between them.

The music started, loud and uncompromising and Anna felt the adrenalin flood through her veins. Looking at Dominic through her lashes, she began to dance. Tentatively at first, growing in confidence as he encouraged her with a smile, a look, Anna moved her body to the music.

After a few minutes she forgot her self-consciousness entirely, moving as one with the music and almost forgetting she had an audience. For the moment Dominic's pleasure was inci-dental to hers. Feeling the beat pound through her veins, Anna was turning herself on.

She was hot, the dress sticking to her skin.

Reaching down she curled her fingers around the hem and, without breaking her rhythm, she pulled it up over her head and threw it to one side.

Dominic's sharp intake of breath reminded her of his presence and she turned to face him. Slowing her movements, she twisted and turned, giving him time to admire her partially clothed body from every angle. He muttered something in French which she didn't understand, though she had no trouble interpreting the expression on his face.

Darting away from his outstretched hand, she laughed, teasing him. Her breasts spilled out of their inadequate restraint as she bent forward from the waist, the rosy, pebble-hard nipples tempting him. At last, just as she was beginning to lose her breath, she slowed her movements, swaying provocatively in front of him.

Sliding off the sofa, Dominic sank to his knees on the carpet in front of her and ran his hands up her legs. His face was level with the soft fur of her pubis and, looking down at the top of his dark head, Anna felt a sudden, intoxicating rush of power. He knelt before her as if in worship, his hands kneading the soft flesh of her buttocks, his mouth close enough to the apex of her thighs for her to be able to feel the warmth of his breath tickling her golden curls.

Tangling her fingers in the thick mass of his hair, Anna urged him to bury his face in the soft centre of her womanhood. The first touch of his lips against her most tender skin made her tremble. Her earlier sense of power was joined now by a peculiar weakness, a heavy, creeping lethargy which made her knees buckle.

Dominic caught her as she slid to the carpet, enclosing her in his arms and easing her up so that he could pull her on to the sofa with him. Anna lay back across his lap, her hair hanging down and pooling on the carpet as he eased her thighs up so that they were resting on his chest, her knees over his shoulders.

Slowly, so slowly Anna felt her nerve endings begin to tingle in an agony of anticipation, he parted her outer labia and ran his thumbs lightly along the moisture-slick grooves of her sex. Patiently he separated and parted each petal of flesh, working the moisture which escaped her along the sensitised skin so that his path was made slippery and wet.

It seemed an age before he was satisfied, an aeon before his lips moved slowly, inexorably towards their target. Anna squirmed, rotating her hips in wild abandon, desperate to feel the heat of his kiss against her exposed flesh.

He didn't kiss her. Instead he darted out his tongue, taking her by surprise as he licked briefly and delicately at the hard nub of flesh which strained towards him.

'Ooh! Oh God . . . please . . . again . . .!'

He was driving her mad with his ticklish caresses, stroking lightly when she wanted to be rubbed hard, moving his tongue back and forth when she wanted him to circle her clitoris . . . was this his way of teaching her not to play with fire?

Mindless with desire, Anna reached for herself, pinching and rolling her desperate flesh between her thumb and forefinger until the first pulse of orgasm began deep in her womb. She moaned as the feathers of sensation radiated outward, consuming her.

Until that moment Dominic had apparently been content to watch at close quarters as Anna wrung a climax from her writhing body. Once the moment was upon her, though, he pushed away her hands and replaced them with his lips and tongue, thrashing the quivering bud where the sensation was concentrated.

Anna whimpered, half in alarm, half in encouragement as his teeth closed gently round it, nibbling at it until she could bear no more and she ground her clitoris against his teeth, wanting, *needing* to feel the pressure against it.

As the strength of the explosion increased, Dominic entered her with his tongue, holding it rigid so that it thrust in and out of her like a miniature penis. Drawing it back and rimming the entrance to her body, he drank her in, lapping at the warm, viscous honey which seeped from her at the point of orgasm.

Anna felt hot, boneless as sensation after sensation spiralled through her. Without realising she was moving, she slid down Dominic's legs so that her head and shoulders were resting on the floor, her legs still wrapped around his body.

His hands came down to grip her hips, anchoring her as she moved to the edge of the chair and thrust into her, burying himself in the soft, honeyed heat of her body. Stretching her arms out either side of her for balance, Anna allowed him to bend her back, so that all her weight was on her shoulders. Standing, Dominic took her weight by holding her behind the knees, leaning over her from the waist in order to increase the depth of his penetration.

He came quickly, his vital seed pumping from him in swift, aggressive spurts. Sinking slowly to his knees, he slipped out of her as he lowered her legs carefully to the ground. Before, she had been too wrapped up in her own ecstasy to notice that her muscles were protesting. Now she brought her knees up to her chest and wrapped her arms around them. Hugging them to her, she welcomed the way in which Dominic wrapped himself, spoon-like, against her back.

His breath was warm against her neck, still laboured and heavy. The knowledge that she had instigated their coming together this time, that she had planned it, carried it out and seen it to its logical conclusion gave her a rare glow of pleasure. It pleased her to know that she could be that powerful, that she had the wiles to seduce and inflame after all.

Lying together in a warm fog of exhaustion and contentment, they fell asleep there, on the living-room floor, locked in an embrace.

Saturday was hot, so hot that the pavements sweltered and the trees stood motionless, waiting for a breeze. Anna pulled out the sun loungers and set them up in the garden so that she and Dominic could doze in the sun, a jug of ice-cold Pimms close at hand.

'I fly home tomorrow,' he said suddenly.

Anna opened one eye and turned her head

towards him. His voice sounded as though it came from far away, suspended on a blanket of heat. Conversation was too much effort, yet she wanted desperately to reply.

'Must you?'

Bending his arm at the elbow, he shielded his eyes from the glare of the sun, trying to read her expression. He looked glorious, stretched out on the lounger, his naked skin bathed in a golden glow. Anna's fingers itched to reach out and touch the crisp black hair which gleamed seal-black in the sunlight, but she resisted the impulse, not wanting to change the tenor of the moment.

He held her eye for a long moment, the lazy, languorous mood dissipated by the thread of tension which stretched between them. It was Dominic who finally dropped his gaze, breaking eye contact.

'I'm afraid I must.' He looked away, across the garden, before bringing his eyes back to hers. 'When Francine suggested you come to my home – you thought I was . . . you have an expression . . .' he clicked his fingers, *'put on the spot'*? I was going to ask you but Frankie was too quick. If I ask you now, myself, will you consider?'

Anna held his eye for a long moment. Finally, she swallowed back the lump which had formed in her throat, saying, 'Yes, I will consider your invitation. Thank you. But I don't want to talk about your leaving. We still have the rest of the afternoon . . . and the night.'

He smiled.

'Yes. Is there anywhere you'd particularly like to go tonight, *chérie*?'

Struck by a sudden mood of gaiety, Anna laughed. 'Yes. I'd like to go dancing.'

'Dancing? *Bon*. Then that is what we shall do!'

He reached for her and they fell together on to the warm, springy turf. His lips, his hands, his voice, all were soft on her senses as he began to love her. Sweetly this time, with none of the urgency which usually characterised their coming together.

Anna found herself twining around him, enclosing him as she would a lover of long standing. Entering her, he loved her so tenderly it brought tears to her eyes. As they came, together, it was as gentle, rolling waves on the shore rather than the usual crashing breakers against the rocks.

Dominic whispered words of love in her ear, stroking her, kissing her ear, her cheek, her neck and Anna knew, beyond all doubt, that this was more than the casual affair she had thought it would be. When he was gone, she would miss him.

They had one more night, one more night when anything could happen. She hung on to that thought as they went back into the house together.

Chapter Eleven

THE DISCOTHEQUE WAS loud and hectic, packed with sweltering bodies, all dancing too closely together. Anna felt Dominic's gaze on her through the strobe lights and she turned to grin at him.

'It's been years since I came to a place like this!' she shouted above the din.

He raised his eyebrows at her. 'And you've missed it?' he asked incredulously.

She laughed and pulled him by the hand on to the crowded dance floor. It felt good to simply dance amongst an anonymous group of people. Anna felt good tonight. She was wearing a white dress with cut-outs at the shoulders and stomach which had been an impulse buy that afternoon. Gold hoops swung from her earlobes, matching the links of the belt which she wore slung low on her hips.

As they had come into the disco she had attracted more than one appreciative glance and the excess of attention had exhilarated her. Now the repetitive, thumping beat made her head feel as though it was filled with cotton wool; it anaesthetised her mind, cleansing it of the creeping sadness which reminded her of Dominic's imminent departure.

It was Dominic who finally dragged her, protesting, off the dance floor.

'Enough!' he shouted, making for the bar, 'I am too old for all this. Come through to the lounge where it is quieter.'

His arm slipped around her waist and urged her forwards to where the lounge area was set back in an L-shaped alcove, away from the noise and bustle of the disco. It was cooler in here as well as quieter and Anna was quite glad to take the weight off her feet. She gulped gratefully at the tall cooling drink Dominic bought for her.

'I'm whacked,' she admitted when he sat down. 'I'd forgotten how exhausting these places can be!'

Dominic laughed and settled back in the seat, his arm resting casually along the top of the upholstered bench behind her shoulders.

There weren't so many people in here, Anna noticed as she looked around her. Generally they were older, most dressed in business suits and cocktail dresses, almost as if they had strayed accidentally into the younger world of the discotheque from the deck of a luxury cruise liner.

On the other side of the room was a door that she hadn't noticed before and now as she watched she saw that most of the older, more smartly dressed people were coming to and from the room beyond.

'I wonder what's through there?'

Dominic picked up his glass. 'Shall we go and see?'

The room beyond was slightly smaller than the larger dance area, but was otherwise a mirror image. Here, though, the music was more middle of the road, the dancers mostly couples.

Finding a seat in the corner, Anna and Dominic sat down and ordered a meal in a basket.

'I like it better here,' he smiled, his eyes crinkling at the corners. 'Here we can talk.'

'Talk? Did you have a particular subject in mind?'

'*Mais oui* – you. And what you are going to do with your life now you have discovered there is more.'

Anna gazed at him, disconcerted by the directness of his question. But then he had always been blunt with her, as if he considered it his right to speak his mind. She minded less than she would have expected and she decided to respond in kind.

'I can't tell you whether or not I will visit you in France, Dominic, at least, not yet.'

He waved a hand dismissively. 'I don't need an answer from you, *chérie*. For what it is worth, I believe you will come. I have to believe that or I would be too sad to leave tomorrow. What I meant was, have you thought about what you want to do with your life?'

Anna smiled. 'I haven't really had time. To be truthful, I haven't given Paul much thought since you arrived. Does that sound awful?'

'Not to me!' he laughed. 'I should have been very upset if you had been thinking about your husband while you have been with me.'

159

Anna reached across and cupped his face with her palm. A rush of tenderness swept over her as she looked at him, an unexpected affection.

'I can't think at all when I'm with you,' she whispered.

Dominic leaned forward so that his forehead rested briefly against hers. His lips brushed, butterfly light, across her lips, his breath warm and sweet.

'Nor I.'

Anna watched as he rose and went to fetch them both another drink at the bar. She liked the way he moved with his long legs striding out, purposeful and yet relaxed. How could she have come to feel so close to him in such a short period of time?

As she watched Dominic, Anna slowly became aware of someone watching her in turn. Turning her head, she saw that there was a group of men sitting at a larger table across the room. Most were engrossed in conversation, but one sat back in his seat, as if wanting to disassociate himself from the others.

He smiled at her across the room when he saw that she had noticed him. Surprised, Anna smiled back. She liked the look of him. He was blond, his hair close-cropped on a well shaped head. Taken individually his features were irregular, certainly not picture-perfect. Yet as a whole his face was attractive and his smile was warm.

'You have an admirer, no?'

Anna started as Dominic sat down with their drinks.

'Don't be silly,' she laughed, picking up her drink and determinedly ignoring the blond man.

Dominic was silent for a few minutes as he drank, though Anna could sense his eyes on her. Finally he leaned forward and whispered in her ear, 'You could have any man in this room.'

Shocked, Anna turned to him. 'What do you mean?'

His eyes signalled his amusement at her reaction, though his tone remained matter of fact. 'You know what I mean, Anna.'

A frisson of sexual energy ran through her as she looked at him. She did know what he meant. With all that she had learned, all that he had taught her, she could seduce anyone. Judging from the attention she had been getting, she must be radiating a confidence that she never had before. The idea shocked and excited her in equal measure.

As if he had been waiting for her to mull over what he had said, Dominic drew her towards him and whispered in her ear. 'The man across the room – the one who was watching you. You could get to know him. Take him back to a hotel room.'

'I . . . I couldn't! He might not want to . . .'

Dominic chuckled softly. 'He wants to. Try it.'

Anna glanced across at the blond man. He was no longer looking at her but had joined in the conversation of his friends.

'You see – he's not even looking at me.'

She sounded more piqued than she had intended and Dominic laughed. 'He might not be looking but he is aware of you. Think of the possibilities, Anna.'

'Yes, he could be a raving lunatic, or have a nasty disease or . . . *anything*. Dominic, you're out

,our mind to suggest I pick up a stranger in a club! And besides,' she added, the tremor in her voice betraying her emotion, 'how can you want me to do it?'

Dominic stroked her hair, pressing his lips against her forehead. 'Would you like me to come with you, *chérie*?'

Anna laughed to cover her nervous tension. 'I don't think he'd like that, do you?'

She felt him shrug. 'He wouldn't need to know.'

Realising that he was serious about his preposterous suggestion, Anna drew away from him so that she could see his face.

'Don't you think he'd notice if you walked into the hotel room with us? I didn't see his white stick!'

'You could let me in when he is in the bed. I could hide in the bathroom until he left.'

'You've got it all worked out, haven't you? Oh, I don't know why we're even discussing this; I'm not doing it and that's that.'

Dominic picked up his drink as if prepared to drop the subject. Anna determinedly ignored the man across the room and watched the dancers instead.

The music was pleasant, but not intrusive and all around them was the low murmur of conversation. She decided she liked the relaxed atmosphere of the place and was happy to sit and drink quietly in the corner. Dominic brought them another round and seemed quite content not to talk any more.

He picked up Anna's hand under the table and

played with her fingers. Massaging her knuckles between his forefinger and thumb, he described small circles in her palm, sending tingles through her arm. Anna closed her eyes, marvelling at how *aware* she was of him all the time she was with him. Always conscious of every nuance of his mood.

Although she had dismissed the idea that she should make love to another man in his presence, it would not stay out of her mind. As the evening wore on and they drank and ate and talked in a desultory fashion, the possibilities kept running through her mind.

Pictures of herself, cavorting naked with another man . . . if Dominic was there she would be safe enough, wouldn't she? Glancing surreptitiously across the room she saw that the blond man she had noticed earlier was still in his seat, though he seemed to have given up on her.

What would it be like to make love with a man just the once, without knowing anything about him at all? The idea intrigued her, made her squirm slightly in her seat. It was dangerous, and yet, if Dominic was there too, safe.

Catching Dominic's eye she realised that he knew what she was thinking about, had probably anticipated that she would mull over the idea in spite of her rejection of it. Suddenly unable to sit still any longer, she leapt up and made for the ladies'.

Once in the cloakrom, she ran her wrists under the cold tap to cool them. Her reflection in the harshly lit mirror above the sink looked pale, though there was a hectic flush to her cheeks.

Surely she couldn't seriously be considering Dominic's suggestion? The sudden dart of tension which ran through her told her that she was. For a few moments she couldn't decide whether she was more excited than frightened.

It was some minutes before Anna felt calm enough to emerge from the sanctuary of the ladies' cloakroom. When she did, it was to find that the room had filled up. Now there were more people milling about and crowding the dance floor. She couldn't see across the room to where Dominic waited for her.

'Would you like to dance?'

She jumped as the voice sounded close to her ear. Turning slowly, she was unsurprised to see the blond man standing close by her. There was a sense of inevitability to the whole scene, an unreality which made it easy to smile and nod.

Close to, Anna saw that he was younger than she had first thought. His square jaw was smooth, not a man who would need to shave twice a day, but no gawky youth either. Blue eyes appraised her with interest, his lips, the bottom one slightly fuller than the top, curved into a smile.

Without saying a word, Anna slipped her hand in his and walked with him on to the dance floor. His skin was warm and dry, his body, she noticed as he drew her into his arms, hard and well toned. Moving with him to the beat of the music, Anna breathed in the subtle, woody tones of his aftershave which overlaid the clean scent of his skin.

She could tell he was already aroused, even though he held her in such a way as to not make it obvious. This gentlemanly touch reassured her and she welcomed the flood of desire which washed through her body. Over his shoulder, Anna could see Dominic now. He was sitting where she had left him, half in shadow. Though she couldn't see his face she recognised the tension in the way he held himself and she hid a smile. It pleased her to please him.

'Have you been here before?' the man with whom she was dancing asked her.

'No,' she replied shortly, unwilling to break into her reverie about Dominic.

'What's your name?'

Anna stepped back slightly and scanned his face.

'Does it matter?'

He looked taken aback.

'Well, I . . . no, I don't suppose it does . . .'

'No names, then. I'd prefer it that way.'

From the way he held her as they resumed dancing, Anna could tell that his bewilderment was overshadowed by his rising excitement. If she hadn't fully engaged his attention before, she certainly had now! She could almost hear the cogs turning in his mind as he tried to figure her out. Was he in with a chance or wasn't he? Anna almost laughed aloud as she thought *if only he knew*!

Wickedly, she pressed herself closer to him, making her intentions plain. His breath quickened, his arms tightening around her body as he rubbed his cheek against her hair. His erection strained against her stomach and he was clearly uncomfortable.

'Would you like to sit down?' he asked her, his voice slightly strangled.

Anna leaned back so that she could look him straight in the face.

'Take me to a hotel.'

His eyes widened momentarily, then darkened. Suddenly he was back in control, almost businesslike. He nodded.

'I know a place.'

'I'll get my bag.'

Dominic wasn't sitting at the table and Anna did not dare to speculate where he might have gone. Part of her hoped he was preparing to follow them in her car, another part of her admitted that she was doing this for herself.

She and the blond man did not speak as they left the club together and made for his car. Anna raised her eyebrows as she saw it. Rare, low slung, sporty – she had obviously picked up a man of means.

He was a good driver, handling the car with unobtrusive competence. Tension trembled in the air between them. He put his foot down. Impulsively, Anna reached over and ran her fingertips lightly from his knee, up his inner thigh to his groin. His left hand clamped over hers, stopping her from enclosing him.

His jaw was set, a small pulse beating in his neck. Smiling to herself, Anna withdrew her hand. The heat and size of his erection seemed imprinted on her palm. She could not wait to get it out, to feel it against her skin . . .

The hotel was small and modern, one of a chain of identical hotels which stretch across the length and breadth of Britain. The receptionist checked them in with a meaningless, glassy-eyed smile and handed the man an electronic disc to open the room.

As they went inside Anna made sure he walked into the room ahead of her so that she could surreptitiously leave the door on the latch, just in case Dominic *had* followed them in her car.

The room was square and modern, spartanly furnished with a double bed, wardrobe and dressing table, but clean. A door off to the right led, she presumed, to the en suite bathroom. Standing with her back against the main door, she watched as the man switched on the lamps which hung over the bedhead. Bathed in a pale orange glow the room looked warmer, less impersonal.

Turning to her, he took off his jacket and tie and laid them on the dressing table stool. Standing very still, he held her eye, as if waiting for something. Anna smiled seductively.

'Take off your shirt,' she whispered, her voice no more than a husky murmur.

He complied and her eyes narrowed in approval as his naked chest was revealed. It was broad and hairless, the nipples like two neat, flat brown discs crowning the swell of his pectorals. Just looking at him, standing semi-naked in the half light, his shoulders held rigid as if poised for fight or flight, sent a dart of pure lust arrowing to the centre of her stomach.

Slowly, very slowly, she walked across the room towards him. He didn't move, though his eyes watched her warily. Inches away from him she stopped. Poking out the tip of her tongue, she moistened her lips. This close, she could feel the moist heat emanating from his body, smell the healthy male sweat which was seeping through his pores.

Reaching out, she ran her fingertips along the line of his collarbone to his shoulder. His skin was hot, almost as if he had a fever, and slightly damp. The flesh was springy beneath her palms as she placed them over the masculine undulation of his chest. Under her right hand, his heart was beating in urgent rhythm, its increased speed a testament to the pitch of his arousal.

Anna felt powerful, in control as she had with Francine. The stranger stood motionless before her, letting her make the advances, offering himself as her plaything. Her very own sex toy. She felt like a child confronted with too many presents on Christmas morning – she didn't know where to begin, what to unwrap first.

Carefully gauging his reactions, Anna slid one hand down, over the tautness of his belly. His expression was inscrutable, though his nostrils flared slightly as his breathing quickened. There was a fine mat of hair which grew in whorls around the deep cleft of his navel, arrowing down beneath it and disappearing into his trousers.

The front of his trousers was pulled taut across his erection, the material creasing under the strain. Looking him straight in the eye, she covered it with her hand and squeezed gently.

A faint sigh escaped through his lips and he shivered.

'You do this often, do you?'

His words were like a slap in the face, a harsh

reclamation of control.

'Do you?' she countered, her fingers hovering uncertainly over his shoulders.

To her relief his face relaxed into a smile.

'Touché,' he breathed, his eyes travelling lazily across her face and down to where her breasts quivered softly, in time with her shallow breathing.

Stepping back slightly, Anna reached behind her and drew down the zip of her dress. Easing it over her shoulders, she pushed it slowly down her body, never taking her eyes from his.

She was naked underneath save for her white lace panties and high-heeled sandals. The man's eyes flickered over her body, his gaze lingering over the voluptuous swell of her breasts. Anna let him look, proud of her body in a way that she never had been proud before.

Lifting his hand, he reached out and stroked the back of his forefinger against one pale pink nipple. It was a touch so light, so barely there, yet it sent an erotic charge tingling right through her, making her toes curl.

The nipple puckered in response to his touch, its twin hardening in sympathy. Glancing assessingly at her, he cupped one breast in each hand, kneading them gently, his hard fingers pressing into the soft flesh. Anna leaned towards him slightly, her eyelids fluttering to a close as his thumbs circled the swollen crests, sending a rush of moist warmth to the centre of her sex.

She could feel her vulva swelling, a heavy, dragging warmth invading the soft labia. In her mind's eye she visualised the folds of flesh growing rosy with anticipation, her clitoris swelling as the slow pulse of desire began to beat at its centre.

Moaning softly, she tangled her fingers in his thick blond hair as he bent his head to take one swollen peak in his mouth. Rolling it on his tongue, he mimicked the action with his fingers on her other breast.

At the back of her mind, Anna thanked goodness that she'd picked up someone who knew what he was doing. But she wasn't prepared to relinquish all control to him. Dragging his head up, she pressed her torso against his while with her fingers she deftly dispensed with the fastening of his trousers and slipped her hand inside.

He groaned as her fingers closed around the tumescent shaft and it jumped in her hand. Anna let it go so that she could take his trousers off. Sliding her body down his so that her nipples glided against the soft hair of his belly, she eased his trousers and boxer shorts over his hips.

His fingers trembled as he helped her, pulling off his socks and shoes as he kicked his trousers to one side. His cock swayed, inches from her face and Anna took it in her hand. It was a handsome specimen, long and thin with a gentle upward curve. Moving her hand up and down the stem a few times, Anna eased back his foreskin to reveal the soft, sensitive skin of his glans.

A drop of clear fluid oozed from the tiny crease at the end and she gave into the impulse to dab at it with her tongue. It tasted salty, slightly warm, and the droplet was quickly replaced by another.

This time she smeared it across his reddening glans with her thumb pad, running the tip of her nail gently along the crease.

With her other hand she cupped his balls, caressing the surprisingly silky hair with her fingertips. His scrotum was warm in her hand, bulging now with his imminent ejaculation. She didn't want it to be *that* imminent, so she let him go, reluctantly, and rose to her feet.

His eyes were slightly glazed, his hair sticking to his forehead. His chest rose and fell with each breath, his lips parted slightly as if he hardly dared to breathe at all.

Taking him by the hand, Anna led him over to the bed. Kneeling on it, in front of him, she put her arms around his neck and pressed herself against him.

He groaned as she rubbed her nipples against his, completely unaware that he was being used, his responses manipulated purely for Anna's satisfaction. The flat discs grew and hardened. Drawing back, Anna pinched them between her thumbs and forefingers, making him gasp.

His cock bounced against the soft swell of her belly, its silky soft skin tickling her. Lying back on the bed she pulled him with her so that he hovered above her, on all fours. Taking his penis between her hands, she worked it slowly, back and forth, until once again it began to seep the thin, clear fluid of pre-emission.

He raised an eyebrow when she produced a condom from her bag but did not object as she rolled it on. It stretched tightly across the breadth of him, the touch of the thin rubber over his sensitive shaft making him swell still more.

Using her upper arms, Anna pressed her breasts together to form a channel between them and urged him to rub himself along her chest. Looking down, she could see the red tip of his cock coming into view then receding as he masturbated himself against her body.

The cords in his neck stood out as his excitement grew, his temperature increasing rapidly. Alarmed that he would not be able to hold back for much longer, Anna called a halt.

'Enough – I want you to make me come first.'

His eyes registered surprise at her forthright request and for a moment she thought that he would refuse. His mouth was set in a mutinous line, his cock fit to burst. Slowly, his tongue snaked through his lips and he licked them.

'That's it,' she crooned, softly, 'use your tongue.'

Maybe he thought she was being too demanding for a one-night stand, for his face registered shock.

'Bitch,' he hissed, though mildly, as if he was more amused than angry.

Holding his eye Anna slowly drew up her knees and let her thighs fall apart. In spite of himself, it seemed, his eyes flickered down to where her sex lay, open and exposed, demanding his attention. A dull flush crept under his skin as, as if drawn by some invisible string, he slowly lowered his head.

At the first sweep of his tongue against her sensitive flesh, Anna shuddered and sank back against the pillows. Up and down went his tongue, licking her grooves with long, leisurely strokes, as if he had all the time in the world.

Closing her eyes, Anna reduced him to no more than a clever tongue, skilful hands and a competent cock. No more than a machine, a sexual cipher, a means by which she could climax. At that moment he had no more of an identity, as far as she was concerned, than a plastic vibrator.

She groaned as the blond nibbled at her clitoris, the sudden, almost painful contact as his teeth grazed her skin tipping her over the edge. Pushing her pelvis towards him, she ground her pleasure bud against his teeth, opening her legs wide and circling her hips.

The intensity of her orgasm took her by surprise. As she struggled to bring it under control, the blond man flipped her over on to her stomach. Lifting her pelvis up, he drove into her still pulsing body, holding her hard against him by placing his hands on her hips and compelling her to be still.

Anna bit the pillow as he fucked her mercilessly, panting with exertion and working himself into a frenzy. It was all over in minutes. Anna sagged as his weight was suddenly removed and she dragged the bed-cover up over her shoulders. The stranger reached to stroke her hair, his fingers trembling as he sought to return to normality.

Suddenly, Anna desired nothing more than for him to go. She didn't want his clumsy attempts at tenderness, she simply wanted to keep their short, annoymous encounter within the boundaries she had set at the beginning. No names, no strings.

He looked as though he would take her in his arms, perhaps kiss her. Drawing back, she gave him a cool smile.

'Would you mind leaving now?'

His jaw dropped for a moment before he recovered enough to try to hid his surprise.

'But—'

'Please. It was lovely, but I feel it's time for you to leave now.'

'You really are a hard little bitch, aren't you? What is it with you – you've used me and now you want to throw me away?'

Anna shook her head.

'Hang on – who used whom? Are you saying you haven't enjoyed it?'

'Of course not!' He frowned, momentarily confused.

'Then I'd say we used each other, wouldn't you?'

For a moment she thought that he was going to argue with her further. He took a breath, then the door clicked and he looked round.

'Bloody hell!'

He looked back at Anna and, seeing that she wasn't as shocked as he to see Dominic lounging in the open doorway, his eyes narrowed.

'Okay – where's the camera?'

'Camera?'

'Yeah. You've obviously set me up. What for? A blue movie?'

Anna put her hand to her mouth and laughed, shaking her head. The man leapt up from the bed and pulled on his clothes, eyeing Dominic warily from the corner of his eye.

'Here,' he took a business card out of his pocket and flipped it on to the bed, 'that's my address so that you can send me my appearance fee. Be seeing you.'

He was out of the door before Anna had time to recover herself. Dominic went over to the door and locked it before picking the card up from the bed and dropping it in the bin without looking at it.

As he approached, Anna realised that his expression was thunderous.

'What's the matter, Dominic?'

'Don't you know?'

Anna frowned, sidestepping what she knew was the real issue.

'Why did you have to come in? That poor man, his face – I thought he was going to have an apoplectic fit!'

Dominic shrugged.

'I didn't want him to outstay his welcome.'

With a flash of insight, she knelt up on the bed, holding the sheet tightly in her bunched fist against her body and faced him.

'You mean you didn't want him to come in at all, don't you?'

A flush of deep colour tinged Dominic's skin as he looked at her. She could sense his tension, taste his anger as it curled around them.

'For God's sake, Dominic, it was your idea in the first place! Don't despise me now for doing as you asked me!'

'I don't despise you, Anna. I just can't stand the thought of him with you, touching you, inside you . . .'

'Then why did you suggest it?'

He raised his hands, palms upwards in a gesture of bewilderment that she found strangely endearing.

'I thought I could bear it. I hadn't realised how . . .'

'How what, Dominic?' she prompted gently when his words tailed away.

His eyes were like two deep, dark pools of desire as he stared at her.

'I hadn't realised how much I have come to care for you,' he said, enunciating each word clearly so that she could not possibly misunderstand him.

In spite of her recent exertions, Anna felt a sudden, savage mule-kick of desire in the pit of her stomach. Dominic faced her, his body held taut, his face set.

'Oh Dominic!' she whispered.

Holding out her arms to him, she waited while he overcame his momentary hesitation and moved towards her.

Chapter Twelve

AFTER THE INITIAL move had been made by Anna, Dominic took full control of the situation. Unwinding the sheet from her body, he ripped off his own shirt, sending buttons flying, so that he could press her against his naked skin. His mouth came down on hers, his lips bruising, fierce in their passion, his fingers tangling in the dishevelled hair at the back of her head.

She moaned as his free hand roamed her body, revelling in his lack of gentleness. There was no place for it this time. His need was to possess, to take what he now regarded as his and to erase the imprint of that other man from her body.

Anna allowed him to bend her and arrange her anyway he chose, welcoming the harsh rasp of his chin against her tender flesh as he sucked and kissed and licked his way down the length of her body.

He was already aroused, as if the thought of her fucking with another man had inflamed him in spite of himself. Jealousy had acted as a powerful spur to his excitement and as his fingers squeezed and kneaded her compliant flesh, Anna was aware of a streak of cruelty in his touch that had been absent before.

'Did he kiss you here?' he asked her savagely, his lips burning a trail from her navel to the sweat-damp hair of her pubis.

Anna moaned incoherently as his tongue snaked into the swollen folds of flesh, probing, stabbing rhythmically at her tender places. His voice was a low, husky murmur as he poured out his anguished imaginings.

'Did he make you come like this?'

Gasping, Anna felt herself drift into an altered state of consciousness as Dominic's tongue began to play with her clitoris. It circled and swirled around it, making it stand proud of its protective hood before teasing it with the lightest touch of the very tip of his tongue.

She could feel the moisture of her arousal welling up and overflowing, bathing Dominic's face in clear, honey-like fluid. When he raised his face, she shrank from his anger.

The taste of her was strong on his lips and tongue as he ground her lips against his teeth. Suddenly, he rose up and shed the rest of his clothes, towering over her like some avenging angel. His penis was sturdily erect, ready to enter her. Sensing his transient need to dominate and control, Anna merely parted her thighs wider to accommodate him.

His first thrust into her body pinned her to the bed. Twisting his hips slightly, he increased the sensation of being skewered, stimulating that elusive, ultra sensitive spot deep inside her vagina which sent ripples of orgasmic sensation chasing through her body from her neck to her toes.

Anna ceased to think in a rational manner. All her attention was focussed on that silky channel of flesh which enclosed Dominic's marauding cock, sucking it in, urging it on to thrust harder, deeper, more quickly. Her arms and legs felt heavy, her head filled with cotton wool, incapable of thought.

Unthinking, her long fingernails dug into his shoulders and raked down his back. This brief savagery provoked him to bite her neck, his teeth nipping an exquisitely painful path across her shoulder to where her breast quivered vulnerably.

Anna whimpered, her arms going up to hold him tighter around his neck, pressing him to her to stop him torturing the soft, tempting globe. They rolled together in a tangled mess of arms and legs, skin sticking together, heat on heat.

Dominic's breath was hot on her face, his teeth flashing white against the tan of his skin as he grimaced, transported to a private plane of pleasure where Anna could only follow. She clung to him as his hips pumped faster.

'Was he good, Anna?' he ground out through gritted teeth. 'Did you like having him inside you?'

Anna moved her head from side to side, too wrapped up in the moving, shivery heat which bathed her body to reply.

'Was he good? Did you feel like this with him? Answer me!'

Anna yelped as he suddenly grabbed her by the chin, bending her head back so that she was forced to look at him. His eyes were glazed, though she

179

thought she recognised the anger in their depths. On the verge of orgasm, she reached up and cradled his face between her hands.

'It's never . . . like this . . . with anyone else, Dominic,' she almost sobbed, 'only you . . . there is only you . . . oh God!'

Her muscles contracted around him as her climax overtook her. Spasm after spasm left her gasping for breath as Dominic took up her rhythm and followed her on the road to ecstasy. He cried out as he came, her name and a stream of endearments in his own tongue. It seemed to go on for ever, a continuous flow of exquisite sensation between them, each setting up a vibration in the other which intensified the original orgasm until they rolled, exhausted, on the crumpled sheets.

Summoning the last of his energy, Dominic drew her to him, moulding her back to the front of his body, spoonwise, his arm holding her tightly to him as if he was afraid to let her go. Within minutes, both were asleep.

They stayed in the hotel room until morning. Somewhere close to midnight Anna woke to find Dominic's hands roaming her body. Burrowing into his warmth, she turned towards him, welcoming the sweet, loving embrace after their altogether more carnal coupling of earlier on.

'Forgive me,' he whispered against her hair.

She pressed her fingertips against his lips.

'Ssh. There's nothing to forgive,' she whispered back.

His eyes mirrored his doubt, spoke of his shame. Taking pity on him, Anna set about convincing him in actions rather than words that she had enjoyed their quasi-violent encounter. Murmuring endearments, she kissed and stroked his chest and belly, running her fingers lightly along the length of his shaft until he trembled with renewed desire.

She didn't need him to touch her, his very nearness, combined with the lingering secretions from a few hours before, meant she was ready for him. Insinuating her right leg beneath his body as he lay facing her, on his side, she guided his penis into the warm, wet solace of her vagina.

His weight was heavy on her right thigh, but the slight discomfort was well worth bearing for the sake of watching his face at such close quarters. His eyelids flickered as he was enclosed by her, his mouth opening on a soft 'O' of pleasure.

Holding his gaze, Anna watched, fascinated, as his pupils dilated until they almost covered the iris and his expression softened. His hands stroked her naked breasts, caressing them almost reverentially.

Unable to penetrate very deeply at this angle, his movements inside her were gentle, more of a rocking motion than a thrust. Little ripples of pleasure feathered their way along Anna's nerve endings and she leaned forward to kiss his parted lips. They were warm and soft, responding languorously to her initiative.

Reaching down, between their melded bodies, Dominic sought the little button of her desire and began to stroke it with his fingerpad. This lightest of touches stimulated her far more than anything more direct could and she sighed deeply, closing her eyes to contain the pleasure.

She opened them again as she felt the tell-tale heat surge through him, wanting to watch his face as he came. There was an almost beatific radiance about his expression as his climax shuddered through him and within seconds Anna came in a gentle, flowing rush which made the whole of her body tingle.

Their foreheads touched, their fingers intertwining beneath the bedclothes. Oblivious now to his weight on her leg, Anna smiled at him before falling swiftly into a deep, contented sleep.

The next time they woke the cool fingers of dawn were playing over the curtains, a cacophony of birdsong breaking the stillness of the air.

'I never dreamed I could behave like this,' Anna mused aloud.

Her cheek was pillowed on Domonic's naked chest, his heart beating its steady rhythm against her ear. He raised his head to look at her.

'Like what, *chérie*?'

Anna made a face as she struggled to find the right words.

'Like . . . like a *strumpet*!'

She laughed, loving the way the old-fashioned word rolled around in her mouth. Dominic's chuckle transmitted itself through his chest, vibrating softly against her cheek.

'If it makes you feel any better, I never thought I could behave like a cuckolded husband.'

Anna pressed her lips against his heart.

'I'm glad you did,' she murmured, her breath gliding over the warm silk of his skin.

They were silent for a while, each content to lie entwined, cocooned from the realities the day would bring. Finally, they could put it off no longer.

'Alan has offered to drive me to the airport,' Dominic told her as they dressed.

'But I thought . . .' Anna bit her lip as she realised how transparent she was being. She had assumed that she would be taking him, that he would want her there when he left. It hadn't occurred to her that he might say goodbye now.

Seeing her stricken expression, Dominic crossed the room and pulled her into his arms.

'Forgive me, *chérie*, but I would rather leave you in your home. I could not bear to walk away from you in the airport.'

Contrarily, Anna longed for the anonymity of Heathrow where she would be forced to contain the tears which, even now, threatened to overflow. Unable to trust herself to speak, she merely nodded, allowing Dominic to interpret her silence as agreement.

The young woman to whom they handed the electronic key was not, thankfully, the same one who had been on duty the night before. Feeling grubby in clothes more appropriate to a night on the town than a sunny summer morning, Anna was glad to reach the sanctuary of her small car. She was relieved when Dominic offered to drive, as she felt battered, physically and emotionally, by the experiences of the night before.

They drove home in silence, leaving Anna too much time to think. One week. That was all the time she had known him, one measly week. Yet in that time she had come to know him, and he her, as she had no one else. And yes, she admitted to herself for the first time, with a little start of surprise, she had grown to love him more than a little too.

Depression settled over her as she busied herself in the kitchen. She could hear Dominic moving about in the guest room upstairs, packing his things. Alan rang the doorbell to let them know he was there, then, refusing Anna's offer of tea, he returned to the car to look through some papers while he waited for Dominic.

When Dominic came downstairs with his case, Anna handed him a small picnic lunch.

'For the journey,' she explained, unnecessarily.

He smiled, that endearing, lop-sided smile which transformed his whole face.

'When does your husband come home?' he asked her unexpectedly.

Ann frowned. 'On Thursday.'

He nodded, glancing down at his feet as if he had been struck by the same awkwardness which now paralysed Anna. When, at last, he spoke again, his voice was soft, but sombre.

'Will you contact me at the weekend? I've left my address and telephone number by your bed.'

Anna nodded miserably.

'Ann-a.'

He whispered her name, drawing out the second syllable as he always did. Looking up, she saw that he had opened his arms to her. With a small cry, she stepped into the warm circle of his embrace, clinging desperately to him as he kissed her face, her neck, her hair.

'*Au revoir*,' he murmured against her ear.

Before Anna could gather her wits to reply he had picked up his case and disappeared through the door, leaving her clutching at formless air.

'Are you sure you're well enough to be here?' Alan paused by Anna's desk on Monday morning and surveyed her white face with concern.

Anna attempted a smile, knowing that she'd failed when Alan drew up a chair and sat down across from her. She had tried to put colour into her face with make-up that morning, but nothing she did seemed to be able to hide the evidence that she had spent hours crying like a lovesick teenager after Dominic's departure.

'You know, I think you might have passed something on to our French friend. He certainly seemed to be sickening for something on the drive to the airport. I've never known him to be so quiet.'

Anna darted a quick look at him from beneath her lashes and saw that he was regarding her shrewdly, a twinkle in his bespectacled eye.

'I . . . I hope not. It would be a shame, wouldn't it . . . I mean . . . did Monsieur Gérard enjoy his trip?' she asked, desperate to talk about him even if in this superficial way.

Alan raised his eyebrows at her. 'Oh I think so. Don't you?'

And she knew then that he knew. Wondering if she should offer some kind of explanation, Anna foundered for a few minutes. Alan surprised her by heading her off.

'When does your husband come home?'

'Thursday,' she replied, startled by his change of tack.

'I see.'

Anna didn't know what it was he thought he saw, but he seemed disinclined to explain. Standing up, he ambled off towards his office. Anna watched him, not sure what to make of the encounter. As he reached the doorway, Alan turned to her and said, 'You've done some sterling work for us here at the college, Anna. Sterling work.'

'Er . . . thank you!' she stammered.

Surely he wasn't going to sack her? For sleeping with her lodger?

'Just remember you're not as indispensable as you might think. People do leave, you know, not always with notice.'

He nodded, as if to himself, before disappearing into his office. Anna gaped after him. Whatever had *that* been about?

The day dragged by after that and Anna was glad to get home. Once inside, though, its emptiness oppressed her, compounding her loneliness. She couldn't be bothered to cook just for herself, so she made a sandwich and a cup of tea and carried them through to the lounge. There was a film on the television, one she had seen before, but it would provide her with company, so she switched it on and curled up on the sofa.

The telephone rang at ten-thirty. Snatching it up, she felt a big, silly grin spread across her face as Dominic's low, sexy voice came across the line.

'You sound as if you could be in the same room!' she marvelled once he had answered her polite questions about his journey.

'I wish I were in the same room, Anna,' he said, his voice growing smoky, sending ripples of delight racing down Anna's spine.

Clutching the receiver more tightly, she closed her eyes, the better to imagine him.

'Tell me what you are wearing, Anna, so that I may pretend I am in the room with you.'

She laughed softly. 'Do you want me to be honest, Dominic, or should I feed your fantasies?'

She could almost feel his warm breath fanning her cheek as he replied. 'Be honest – you are my fantasy, *chérie*, even if you are wearing a sack!'

'It's not that bad! I changed when I got home from work, and now I'm wearing black track shorts and a plain, cream-coloured T-shirt.'

'Shoes?'

'No, bare feet.'

'How are you wearing your hair?'

Without thinking, Anna raised her hand and smoothed the loose top-knot she had created for coolness when she changed after work.

'I've pinned it up . . . it's so hot . . .'

'Take out the pins. I love it when it's loose, falling about your shoulders like a golden shawl. Shake it out so that I can imagine I am running my fingers through it.'

His voice was low and hypnotic, caressing her senses across the miles. Without being aware that she had done so, Anna drew out each hair pin and let them drop soundlessly to the carpet, one by one, as he spoke. Smoothing her hair over her scalp, she played absently with each tress, winding it round her fingers and stroking it across her cheek.

'Sit down, Anna, and relax.'

'How did you know I was standing up?'

His chuckle was warm. 'Because you always stand by the little mahogany table by the window when you answer the telephone. Are the curtains closed?'

'Yes.'

'*Bon*. Sit on the sofa, the long sofa with the soft cushions that you like to put at your back. Are you comfortable? *Oui*? Put up your feet – is that the TV I can hear in the background? Pick up the remote control and turn it off, *chérie*.'

In the back of her mind, Anna wondered why she was allowing herself to be directed like a stringless puppet over the telephone. But then, she knew why – this was Dominic and for Dominic she would do almost anything. He was speaking again now and she forced herself to concentrate on his words as well as the sound of his voice.

'What are you wearing underneath your shorts and T-shirt?'

'Um, just panties.'

'White lace panties?'

'No, pale pink – silk.'

'No bra?'

Anna squirmed slightly on the sofa.

'It's too hot for a bra,' she explained, slightly defensively.

'It is? Or are *you* too hot to wear one?'

Anna laughed, feeling the heat creep under her skin in spite of herself. Although his tone was light, his words were strangely compelling.

'If I were with you now I would slip my hand under your clothes and feel how fast your heart is beating. Can you feel it, Anna?'

With a start of surprise, Anna realised that she had placed her hand beneath her left breast, against her heartbeat.

'Anna?'

'I . . . yes, I can feel it,' she said, her voice small.

'How does it feel?'

'Erratic.' She swallowed, finding her throat unusually dry. 'My skin is hot . . .' she trailed off, taken aback by the strength of her arousal.

'Yes, Anna?' he prompted, his voice thick with desire.

'My . . . my breast is heavy . . . swollen . . . I want . . .'

'Tell me, Anna, tell me what it is you want?'

'Only that you be here . . . to touch me.'

'Oh Anna, if only I could! Let me tell you what I would do if I *was* there with you, then you can touch yourself as I would touch you and I will share with you the pleasure.'

'Yes,' she breathed, her eyes half closing as she imagined his bigger, harder hands supporting the weight of her breast.

'Feel the nipple, Anna – is it hard?'

'Mmmm!'

'And the other?'

'Oh ye-es!'

Pushing the phone beneath her chin and both hands beneath her T-shirt, Anna rubbed her breasts with the flat of her hands, feeling the hard little nubs of her nipples pressing into her palms.

'Does that feel good?'

His voice, smoky with desire, added another layer to her pleasure, cocooning her in warmth.

'You must be very hot now, Anna. Are you hot?'

'Mmm, yes I am. I am hot.'

'Take off your shorts – kick them over to the other side of the room. Have you done that?'

'Yes. I'm sitting here now in just my panties and T-shirt, caressing my breasts so that they ache for your touch, your kiss . . . oh Dominic! I hadn't realised how much I would miss you!'

'I know, *chérie*,' he soothed, 'but I am with you in all but body – you can be my body! Do you know what I would do now, if I was there?'

Anna smiled.

'I think you would slip your hand between my legs and feel the heat of me through my pink silk briefs. And what you felt would make you tremble,' she whispered wickedly as she enclosed the hot, wet silk in her hand.

Dominic was silent for a long moment, though she fancied she could hear him breathing. When he finally spoke, his voice sounded hoarse.

'Are you wet, *chérie*?'

'Mmm, very wet. I'm taking off my panties now because I'm so uncomfortable . . . oh Dominic, they're sodden!'

She smiled to herself as she heard him curse under his breath. Sensing a subtle shift in power, she trailed her fingers languidly along the warm, wet creases of her vulva and sighed.

'I ache, Dominic, a heavy, dragging ache between my legs . . . I wish you were here so that you could kneel between my legs and soothe me with your tongue . . .'

'Stroke yourself, *chérie*, ah, if I close my eyes I can see you there, behind my eyelids! What a sight you are, so beautiful, so *open* to me!'

As he spoke, Anna moved her fingers slowly across her sensitised skin, teasing a reaction from it. Lying back on the sofa, she spread her legs wide, manipulating the many folds of flesh with ease until her breath was coming in short, sharp staccato.

'Can you feel it building, Anna?'

'Oh yes!'

'Then I know your head is flung back, your mouth stretched wide, your eyes glazed. There is a pink flush creeping under the skin of your chest and neck. You breasts are out-thrust, tempting me to touch and taste . . . am I right, *chérie*?'

Realising he had described her position exactly, Anna was unble to do more than murmur an incoherent consent.

'I can feel the warmth of your skin in my hands, can feel the delicious weight of each breast. The jewel between your thighs gleams with your juices. I can smell you, Anna, on my fingers, taste you on my lips! Such perfume, such exquisite flavour – it will stay with me always.'

She began to moan softly, her fingers working in greater rhythm as her clitoris strained and throbbed.

'That's it, Anna, enjoy yourself! Slip your fingers inside yourself . . . can you taste them?'

She did, licking at the piquant, pearly fluid which coated her fingers as if it was the finest caviar. Imagining Dominic's dark head was between her thighs, his lips feasting on her, she almost dropped the telephone.

'Oh, oh God, Dominic it's coming – I can feel it
. . . oh, oh, ooh!'

The orgasm washed over her in wave after
heated wave, bathing her skin in perspiration.
Dominic's voice purred in her ear, whispering
crude endearments which intensified her frenzy.

Afterwards she felt limp, totally drained.

'Anna? Anna, are you all right?'

With an effort she stirred herself to reply.

'Mmm . . . oh, Dominic, this is when I need you
most, to hold me, to fill me up . . .'

'Don't take too long, my love, to make up your
mind to come to me. Long distance sex is all very
well, but as you say, the afterglow is a little cool
when spent alone! Go to bed now.'

'Will you phone tomorrow?'

'I have to go away for a few days, to Paris. I'll
call you on Thursday when I get back, *oui*?'

Anna wanted to protest that there were
telephones in Paris too, but something stopped
her. What right had she to make demands on
Dominic when she herself could not even sort out
her own marriage?

'Until Thursday, then.'

'*Au revoir*, Anna.'

'*Au revoir*, Dominic.'

She replaced the receiver as carefully as if it had
been made of cut glass. Imagining Dominic doing
the same on the other end, she wondered if he
had come too, all those miles away. If so it must
be the ultimate in safe sex! Smiling to herself, she
acted on Dominic's suggestion that she take
herself off to bed.

It was only as she was slipping between the cool cotton sheets that she realised that Thursday was the day that Paul was due to return home. She shrugged slightly. What was the point of her worrying about his reaction to a telephone call when she was contemplating leaving him altogether?

Hugging her pillow to her, she pushed all thought of her husband to the back of her mind. It was Dominic she wanted with her now and it was Dominic's face which danced behind her eyelids when, at last, she fell asleep.

Chapter Thirteen

ANNA WAS ABOUT to leave for work the following morning when the telephone rang again. She was delighted to recognise Francine's seductive tones.

'Frankie! How are you?'

'I'm fine but I was thinking that maybe you would be feeling a little sad now that Nicky has gone, no?'

Anna smiled into the telephone.

'A little,' she admitted with masterful understatement.

'I thought you might want some company – would you like to go out tonight?'

'Tonight? Well, I—'

'Come to London, Anna. I feel like painting the town red and I need some help.'

Anna laughed.

'Put like that, how could I refuse?'

And so it was that she found herself dashing home from work to shower and change before making for the station. Frankie had given her little idea of where they were going, but had warned her to wear something black. Intrigued, Anna had dressed in a short black skirt and figure hugging jacket, adding a scarlet T-shirt underneath for effect.

She had to admit, she looked good. Her long, black-stockinged legs looked slim as they emerged from the short skirt, her gold-blonde hair lay in fashionably tousled disarray about her shoulders.

Frankie met her at the station.

'Anna! Anna – over here!'

She waved happily, though she had no need to for as soon as Anna looked in her direction she spotted her amongst the commuters milling about on the concourse. In minuscule black tube dress and white hold-ups which couldn't quite decide whether they were exceptionally long socks or short stockings, Frankie was attracting a fair amount of attention. Her straight black hair hung in a line down her back, her make-up immaculate as always. Rushing up to Anna, she kissed her twice on each cheek before drawing back to scan her face.

'Not as lonely as expected, *chérie* – surely you have not found someone else already?'

Anna laughed and told her about Dominic's telephone call.

'So you see, I've barely had a chance to miss him yet!'

Frankie was delighted with the tale, making Anna re-tell it as they hailed a taxi and climbed inside.

'How like Nicky! The next time he calls you will

be able to tell him all about your experiences tonight.'

'Experiences?' Anna echoed in alarm.

'Perhaps you will be a watcher tonight – whatever, I think you will find Liginey's very interesting.'

She would say no more, perhaps sensing that Anna was as uneasy as she was intrigued. What was this place where Francine was taking her?

They drew up in front of a nondescript-looking restaurant in a quiet back street near Kensington High Street. This in itself was a surprise to Anna. She had expected to be in Soho, not in the genteel environs of this leafy road!

Paying the taxi driver, Frankie smiled at Anna and led her down a narrow stairway to the cellar. As she passed the white painted gatepost, Anna saw that there was a discreet brass plaque fixed to one, like a doctor's or a dentist's, with the name Liginey engraved on it.

Someone had made an effort to make the small area which led off from the steps clean and welcoming and terracotta tubs of petunias stood sentry either side of the matt black door.

Frankie lifted the brass door knocker and waited. Anna could feel a slight vibration under her feet, realising with a start that the club must actually be in the cellar. Seeing her puzzled expression, Frankie explained, 'This entire row of houses is owned by Louis Liginey and his organisation. The cellars have been converted to make the club.'

Anna raised her eyebrows. About to ask Frankie more, she was prevented by the arrival of a tuxedo-clad man who opened the door and stepped outside. He was as broad as he was tall, his bullet-shaped head too small for his body, as if put there as an afterthought. On recognising Frankie, his forbidding features relaxed into a toothy grin.

'Mademoiselle Didier – and a friend? Please, come in.'

Anna smiled uncertainly as she followed Frankie inside. The man's voice was unexpectedly refined, curiously at odds with his Neanderthal appearance. He grinned at Anna as she glanced sidelong at him, obviously aware of, and amused by, her confusion.

To her surprise, the corridor opened out into a room very similar to the nightclub where she had danced with Dominic a few nights before. Several white-clothed tables were arranged around a small, parquet dance floor where some half dozen people were moving slowly to the music played by the DJ in the corner. A bar ran along the far wall, each of its tall stools occupied. The lighting was dim so that there were several dark corners and shadowy recesses impenetrable to the casual eye.

The man who had let them in showed them to a table and leaned over so that his face was close to Frankie's.

'The usual, *mademoiselle*?' he asked.

Frankie smiled her assent and he headed towards the bar. He seemed to know everyone for his progress was hampered by people greeting him. Raising a casual hand to some, stopping to pass a few words with others, he eventually reached the bar and Anna lost sight of him.

'He is an interesting man, no?' Frankie said, smiling at Anna's interest.

'Who is he?'

'That, my darling, is the great Liginey himself.'

'But I thought—'

'That he was the doorman?' Francine shrugged her narrow shoulders. 'He will be pleased. Tonight he *is* the doorman. Louis likes to be different people. I have this theory that he is a frustrated actor.'

Anna raised her eyebrows, intrigued. She looked at the man through new eyes as he came back carrying a silver ice bucket from which poked a bottle of champagne.

'On the house,' he told them, popping the cork with a flourish and filling their glasses.

He waved away Anna's thanks with a languid hand which belied his bullish appearance before disappearing into the crowd.

'Well, what do you think?' Frankie asked as they had both sat and sipped their champagne for a few minutes.

Anna shrugged.

'Of the club? To be honest I'm a bit disappointed. I expected it to be a little more . . . risqué, I suppose!'

Francine laughed, clapping her hands together with delight.

'Oh Anna! Look around you, *ma chère* – all is not as it seems! Take those women over there as an example.'

Anna followed Frankie's gaze. At the corner of the bar a group of three women were clustered together, eyeing the dance floor and giggling

amongst themselves. If Francine hadn't suggested she should look more closely, Anna's eyes
would have passed over them quite quickly. Now
she studied them, noticing their large hands,
bouffant hair and overdone make-up. They were
taller than average women too and there was
something about the way they were holding
themselves . . .

'They're men, aren't they?'

Frankie laughed at Anna's surprise and pointed
discreetly into the shadows opposite them.

'It is not that simple, *chérie*.'

It took a few moments before Anna's eyes
became well enough accustomed to the gloom to
see the outlandish costumes worn by a large
number of the clientèle. Black, PVC bondage suits
vied with little leather numbers. In many cases,
gender differences seemed to Anna to be blurred.

One girl appeared to be wearing nothing but a
furry bikini and a leather collar round her neck
from which was attached a long, thin lead.
Whoever was holding the end of the lead was
hidden from Anna's view by a statuesque blonde
whose eyes roamed restlessly about the room.

'What *is* this place?' Anna asked her friend as
she quickly averted her eyes as the blonde
woman's gaze found her and her face lit up with
sudden interst.

Frankie laughed.

'It's a club, Anna. A very exclusive club, for
people with very particular tastes. Come – drink
up and I'll show you around.'

Edging their way round the dance floor, Anna
hid a smile at the sight of a middle-aged man

proudly wearing nothing but a white net tutu. Taking more interest in her surroundings, Anna saw that there were wide corridors radiating out from the dance area. Frankie headed off along one, flashing a smile over her shoulder at Anna.

Intrigued, Anna followed. There were doorless rooms leading off from the corridor, each with a crowd of people at the entrance. Pausing to see what was going on in the first room she came to, Anna's jaw dropped, her eyes popping.

There was nothing in the room except for a large, square, metal-topped table. A woman was stretched across it, her head hanging down over one end so that her long, red hair swept the floor. A man was standing, thrusting his penis into her upside-down mouth whilst, at the other end, a second man had buried his face between her bare, white thighs.

The tension in the room was palpable as all the watchers in the room concentrated on the escalation of the participants' pleasure. On the other side of the table, a man was masturbaing himself furiously. As Anna watched, he came, spurting thick, white jets of sperm all over the woman's breasts, making her body squirm.

This appeared to be too much for one of the women watching. With a small, anguished cry, she dived under the table, took the penis of the man who was licking the woman and put it in her mouth.

Anna turned away, disturbed. She had never dreamed that such debauchery took place. Looking around her, she tried to locate Frankie in the milling crowd, but she was nowhere to be seen. For want of anything else to do, she walked slowly along the corridor, her eyes alert for Francine's dark head.

In a room to her right she saw a fairly mundane coupling featuring a pot-bellied, middle-aged man. He was laying on his back, on the floor, while a young woman with short, spiky hair rode him like a horse. Up and down she went so that the man's thick, dark-skinned penis came into view, shiny with the moisture from her body, then disappeared again as she plunged back down on him.

When Anna finally found Francine, her jaw dropped in amazement. Frankie had wandered into one of the tableaux and appeared to have taken it over. Standing erect, hands on hips, her white-stockinged legs akimbo, she had a young, broad-shouldered man on his knees in front of her, as if paying homage. He appeared to have a tireless tongue, oblivious to all the onlookers as he darted it in and out of Francine's out-thrust vulva.

Catching Anna's eye over the heads of the small crowd who had gathered, Frankie winked. Her eyes closed as she gave a brief, orgasmic shudder, then she brought up her foot and kicked the man away. Anna gasped as the young man was sent sprawling on the floor.

'What the hell was that supposed to be?' Frankie told him scornfully. 'You couldn't turn any woman on with a performance like that!'

The man cringed on the floor, though, Anna noticed, his pale eyes were avid. Though his limbs trembled as Frankie had him hauled to his feet and spread face down on the table, his eyes followed her every move, like a faithful dog.

Anna watched with horrible fascination as Frankie took up the whip that was passed to her and brought it down across the young man's naked buttocks. He howled, his hips pumping convulsively against the table as Frankie delivered another blow. Clearly enjoying herself, Francine ordered one of the women watching to take the young man's cock in her hand.

'Tell me when he's ready to come, so that I can whip him harder,' she cried.

This Francine was so unlike the soft, malleable creature with whom Anna had made love that she turned away, confused. It didn't turn her on to see a man sexually humiliated. Something else she had found out about herself – that kind of domination left her cold.

Wandering through the labyrinthine corridors which wound their way through the cellars, Anna felt as if she was trapped inside some kind of bizarre, surreal landscape. She didn't belong there, didn't understand what drove these men and women to such extremes of pain and degradation. Some of the tableaux she unwillingly witnessed could more accurately be described as scenes of torture.

Turning a corner, her eye was caught by a statuesque redhead who was standing astride the large metal table which seemed to feature in every room. Her eyes were covered by a half mask in black leather which fitted snugly over the bridge of her nose. Her full, reddened lips were twisted into a sneer of contempt for the man who lay, fettered hand and foot, beneath her.

Anna strained her neck over the crowds to see him, but could only catch a glimpse of his outstretched body, his penis standing ramrod straight, unregarded and unattended. He was clearly very near to climax and, for a moment, Anna almost felt sorry for him. Reminding herself that this was undoubtedly a predicament of his own making, Anna turned her attention back to his tormentor.

The woman was dressed in a kitschy black leather basque, studded with silver spikes which narrowed her waist to ridiculous proportions. Her large, creamy-skinned breasts were pushed up so that they spilled over the top of the corset, their large crowns rouged a shocking shade of red. Naked from the waist down, she was wearing spike-heeled PVC boots, laced from ankle to knee.

In her hand she was holding a large glass, filled with what looked like water, from which she drank frequently. As soon as the glass was finished, someone stepped forward and refilled it so that she could continue drinking.

Her pubic hair was bushy, an unusual dark red in colour. From where Anna stood, looking up at her from the back of the crowd, she could see the dark red folds of her vulva, dry as far as she could tell, almost menacing in their openness.

As Anna watched, the woman bent her legs slightly at the knees, so that she was squatting over her hapless victim's face. Her lips twisted into a smile before, to Anna's total disbelief, she suddenly let go of a stream of urine.

A collective sigh arose from the watching

audience, only Anna's gasp held a hint of shock. The stream seemed to go on and on, filling the enclosed space with its pungent odour as it hissed and steamed against the man's quivering skin. From the woman's position Anna realised it must have hit him directly in his face. Within seconds, he came.

Straining forward, Anna was seized by a sudden urge to see the man's face, to gauge his reaction to what seemed to her to be a most extreme humiliation. His eyes were closed, his mouth stretched wide as he sought to catch the last drops of urine. It was then she recognised him. His name whispered over her lips.

'Paul . . .!'

Shocked to the core, she turned away from the spectacle of her husband's dripping face, and ran.

Chapter Fourteen

ANNA WAS SHAKING by the time she found Francine. Even now she could scarcely credit that it was Paul she had seen further along the corridor. Although a part of her felt it absurd that she should harbour such thoughts, she felt betrayed by her discovery. As if she were somehow tainted by it. *How could he?*

Frankie was thoroughly enjoying herself with the young man she had been whipping earlier. When Anna found her she was busy moving a vibrator in and out of his anus while the woman she had picked earlier diligently sucked at his cock. The man was sobbing, almost incoherent with gratitude for this rough handling. After what she had just seen, Anna felt nothing for him but contemptuous disgust.

'Francine!' she hissed loudly.

Frankie looked up in surprise, pausing in her action so that the man whimpered pathetically. Ignoring him, Frankie's eyes signalled a question. Seeing the look on Anna's face, she walked away, leaving the dildo vibrating madly in his backside with no one at the helm. Despite her distress, Anna could not help but notice that Frankie didn't look back once.

'What is it, *chérie*? You look terrible!'

'I can't explain, Frankie, not here. I have to go . . . I just wanted to tell you I was leaving . . .'

'But I must drive you to the station, no?'

'Please, Frankie, don't leave on my account—'

'*Merde*, Anna, I wasn't having *that* much fun! I'll drive you home, if you like, then you will have the chance to tell me what it is that has upset you.'

Startled, Anna protested, 'But it's miles out of London, Frankie, and a long way from your home . . .'

Francine shrugged, steering Anna through the crowds to the cloakroom where they retrieved their jackets.

'Maybe you could put me up for the night. I don't need to work tomorrow, and something tells me you won't want to spend the night alone.'

They were in the street now and before Anna had time to protest, Frankie had found them a cab which sped them to where she had parked her car.

During the journey home, Anna related what she had seen to Frankie. Indignant, ashamed, she poured out her shock and her fury as the other girl listened in silence. When she had finished, Anna relaxed back in her seat for the first time, exhausted. A few minutes passed before she felt strong enough to glance at Francine.

Her delicate profile was turned away from her,

her long, dark hair providing a screen for her expression. Only the slight shaking of her shoulders gave her away.

'Francine? Frankie – it's not funny!'

Outraged that this girl whom she had thought was her friend could actually laugh at her anguish, Anna was distraught. She watched in disbelief as, as if unable to hold it in any longer, Frankie allowed the laughter to bubble to the surface. Turning her face to Anna, she saw her expression and tried vainly to control herself.

'Oh, Anna, I'm so sorry! *Merde*, I am not laughing at you. It's just the thought of that insensitive, boorish man you have told me about getting his kicks from a golden shower ... doesn't it make you feel better about yourself?'

'Better . . .?'

'You know – more free? After all, you don't have to respect him any more.'

Anna felt her anger recede as she understood what Frankie was trying to tell her. Gazing out of the window, she watched the darkened countryside flash past, a background to the vivid visual memory of Paul tethered to the metal table.

In all the years they had been married she had never once seen him lose control. Yet as that woman had emptied her bladder all over him he had reacted with a spectacular lack of self-regard which rendered him virtually unrecognisable to her.

He had always seemed so sure of himself, had always insisted that he be the one to initiate any sexual congress between them. Even then, his reactions to their short, sterile couplings had borne no relation to the debauched ecstasy he had exhibited earlier.

Squirming slightly in her seat, Anna recalled how insistent he had always been that she should lie still throughout, as if he didn't want to be reminded of her presence whilst he thrust in and out of her. Treating her as a receptacle for his lust rather than as the living, breathing woman who shared his life.

Now she wondered what he had been thinking of as he used her unresponsive body. Or whom. Had he been imagining the joy of subjugating himself to another woman even while he was spilling his seed into his unsuspecting wife? Accusing her of frigidity because she hadn't a clue what his sexual leanings really were?

If Dominic hadn't happened along at this particular stage of her life, she might have always believed it was some failing within herself which meant she couldn't satisfy him. Paul had almost convinced her that she was the one who was lacking, whose sexual urges were out of the ordinary.

Frankie was right, it *was* funny. Sad, but hilariously so, and at last Anna was able to find release in laughter. Francine joined in, clearly relieved that Anna was not offended by her reaction after all.

'You should have seen him, Frankie! My clean-cut, pompous husband paying someone to piss all over him! If only he'd asked, I'd have done it for nothing! Bastard!'

Later, the tears came, mingling with her laughter. She was glad of Frankie's presence in her bed, though nothing of a sexual nature had happened between them. The other girl's presence was a comfort as she cradled Anna in an almost sisterly embrace, stroking her hair and encouraging her to talk.

'He made me think I was abnormal, Frankie. I can't forgive him for that. Why couldn't he just admit we weren't compatible? Given me the chance to find happiness with someone else?'

She felt Frankie's shrug.

'He is a man, *chérie*. Few men will admit to failure.'

'Failure?'

'*Oui*. He must have intended to suppress his true nature when he married you. *He* failed, Anna, not you.'

Anna frowned.

'I suppose so.'

They lay in silence for a while, and Anna replayed the sad story of her marriage in her head. All those wasted years. It wasn't as if their relationship was good outside the bedroom. She had never realised quite how barren their lives had become until now; it was as if seeing Paul in his true colours had ignited a torch paper in her mind, lighting up the darkest recesses.

'What am I going to do?' she wailed, suddenly overcome with fear.

Francine's lips skimmed her forehead.

'You are going to survive,' she said firmly, 'to move on. Have you forgotten Dominic?'

'Forgotten him? No, of course not. But if I go to him, it can't be purely because I leave Paul. I can survive on my own.'

'Of course you can, *chérie*. But you are forgetting that Dominic loves you. Don't reject him because you are angry with Paul.'

Anna was silent for a while as she digested this new perspective. Francine was right, there was a very real danger that her anger at her discovery would colour how she thought about everything.

'What about you . . . and Dominic?' she asked suddenly.

Francine's fingers stilled in their rhythmic stroking for a moment. She answered slowly, resuming the caress as she did so.

'Nicky is a very good friend. I love him, but not in the way that you love him. There is something . . . special between the two of you that I don't think Dominic has found before.'

'Do you mind?' Anna whispered, a thrill of delight running through her at Frankie's words.

'*Non, chérie.* You are good together and I am happy. I have a feeling that I won't be as close to either of you again as before, but, *c'est la vie, n'est-ce pas*? No hard feelings.'

They fell silent again, each wrapped up in her own thoughts. Anna smiled to herself as she thought of Dominic. Though he had taken her to the very limits of sensual experience, he had never treated her with anything but respect. No matter what they were doing, no matter how extreme, she had always felt safe. With Paul she had never experienced that emotion. Every encounter had been an ordeal, every coupling an exercise in misery.

Did he have any idea, any inkling of how she felt? Did he never spare a thought for her whilst he was playing out his fantasies with his mistresses? Maybe he wouldn't understand the shame she felt. After all, humiliation was his pleasure, wasn't it?

At once it became clear to Anna what she must do to regain her self-respect. A new sense of purpose surged through her as she explained to Frankie what she intended to do.

'Maybe then I'll go to Dominic,' she concluded, 'but only on my terms. The only person who can dictate to me from now on is me.'

Francine's topaz eyes glowed appreciatively at her in the semi-darkness.

'Bravo, *chérie*. I know you will make the right decision – both for you and our dear Dominic. Will you allow me to help you prepare for Paul's homecoming on Thursday?'

Anna leaned forward and kissed her gently on the cheek.

'I would be very glad of your help, Frankie,' she whispered, 'just as I am glad of your company tonight. Now I think we'd better get some sleep – we have some serious shopping to do between now and Thursday!

Paul pulled his car into the driveway and killed the engine, sitting for a few moments before summoning up the will to open the car door. He was always overcome by this awful, deadening emotion at the prospect of going into his own home, confronting his wife.

No doubt Anna would be waiting for him, dutifully demure in a Laura Ashley print. Her mouth would be smiling, even while her wide, grey eyes followed him around the room, silently accusing him. He sighed. It was all becoming too tiresome. And the strain was beginning to tell on him. Why else would his need have increased so dramatically lately? His obsession become so urgent, so difficult to control?

Aware that Anna would have heard the crunch of his tyres on the gravel drive, he quickly got out and locked the door. The thought that she might come out of the house to see what was keeping him made him hurry.

Normally when he arrived home after one of his 'trips', Anna would make sure she was waiting for him with a home-cooked meal, maybe even candles on the table, an expression on her face which always reminded him of a pleading puppy. It always made him feel as if he wanted to kick her. Sighing heavily, he turned his key in the lock and pushed open the door.

The vision which greeted his eyes as he went reluctantly into the living-room made him stop in his tracks. Anna was waiting for him all right, but without a single scrap of flowery fabric in sight.

She was standing in the middle of the room, legs akimbo, fists planted firmly on her hips. A black leather corset bound her from breast to thigh, nipping in her waist so tightly that his fingers itched to touch her, to see if, as he suspected, his hands could span her waist.

Apart from the corset, she was naked, no stockings, just a pair of laced, spike-heeled ankle boots which, combined with the way she had wound her long, gold-blonde hair on the top of her head in a tight coil, made her appear impossibly tall. Just looking at those dangerous little boots gave him an instant erection. Consequently, when he finally spoke, his voice came out an octave higher than was normal.

'Anna! What have you done to yourself?'

He had time to notice the way her lips curled into a sneer before his eyes were drawn irresistibly to the light fuzz of blonde pubic hair visible between her legs.

'Shut up, Paul.'

His head shot up in shock as she spoke. Her voice was so calm, so controlled, so utterly compelling that he felt himself begin to tremble.

'I . . . I don't understand . . .'

'Don't you?' she smiled unpleasantly and for the first time he noticed she was holding a riding crop in her fist. He almost came in his pants, there and then.

'Get upstairs, Paul – I want to hear how your trip went.'

A small voice in the back of his mind told him to get a grip, to stop this ridiculous charade now, before it was too late. He ignored it. Welcoming the rush of sexual heat which turned his legs to jelly, he turned slowly towards the stairs and climbed them with blind obedience.

Anna watched as Paul walked up the stairs in front of her, stunned that her performance had been so spectacularly successful. That he was excited was obvious and the air around them seemed to vibrate with the strength of his arousal. She had to admit, his immediate capitulation to her will was something of a turn-on. Frowning, she reminded herself that that wasn't the idea. She wasn't meant to enjoy it, had to keep a clear head at all times if her plan was to be seen through to its conclusion.

'Undress.'

It seemed the direct approach was best. Watching through narrowed eyes, she noticed how his fingers trembled as he fumbled with his shirt buttons. She wasn't going to help him, that wasn't part of the plan.

Waiting until he was completely naked, she stood tapping the toe of her boot impatiently on the carpet, noticing how this small manifestation of her displeasure increased his excitement still more. To think that all these years she had never even suspected what made her husband's sexual clock tick!

Resisting the urge to laugh, she flicked the tip of the riding crop against her thigh, just hard enough to make a small slapping sound. Paul looked at her wide-eyed, apparently unable to utter a single word.

His body looked well-toned and tanned, though his penis bobbed up and down in front of him, a white, uncontrollable baton, so different in skin tone to the rest of him that it looked as though it belonged on another body. With a flick of her riding crop, Anna indicated that he should climb on to the bed.

He did so, though he chose that moment to speak.

'Anna, I don't know what it is that you think you know about me, but I can assure you – ah!'

'Shut up!' she snapped as she passed the crop

over his buttocks.

'But—'

'You're not to speak unless you're spoken to. Understand?'

For a moment she thought that he was going to argue with her, but after a while a strange expression crept into his eyes and he lay, acquiescent as a bride, on his back on the bed.

'Yes,' he whispered, his voice hoarse.

'Yes *what*?' Anna snarled, looming over him menacingly.

Paul's eyes closed momentarily and his Adam's apple moved in his throat as he swallowed convulsively.

'Yes – *Mistress*,' he croaked.

Anna was amazed at the speed with which he had accepted her authority. The costume had obviously helped, just as Frankie had said it would . . .

'Spread your legs and arms.'

She was gratified to see the flicker of doubt which ran through his eyes as he obeyed her. Fetching the assortment of scarves and ties she had found earlier, Anna set about binding him securely by the wrists and ankles to all four corners of the bed.

Francine had shown her which knots to use so that he couldn't wriggle free. She had practised on her own ankles until she was sure that she could tie a secure knot – she was determined that Paul should be aware that she was very serious in her intentions.

Watching the fear chase itself across his features as he gave an experimental tug on one of his bonds, Anna knew that he was very aware now that this was for real.

How must he feel, lying there so vulnerably? Stepping back to admire her handiwork, Anna smiled to herself. He really had no idea, even now, what was in her mind. Eyeing her warily, his eyes glazed with lust, he could not imagine the hours she had spent planning for, anticipating this moment.

His penis stood at right angles to his groin, a slim, white column swaying slightly as he strained to keep his eyes on her as she walked around the bed. Reaching across, she enclosed it in her fist, running her hand up and down several times in fast succession until he groaned aloud.

'Hmm,' Anna said, removing her hand, 'I see you have no respect for your mistress.'

'Oh but I do! Please, Anna – I mean, Mistress, please allow me to come . . .'

'Allow you to come?' Anna allowed her eyebrows to rise in contempt. 'And what makes you think you deserve to be relieved?'

Paul's breathing was growing harsher as he tried to control his excitement. A fine film of sweat rose on his flesh as she climbed carefully on to the bed and stood astride him, as she had seen the redhead do at Liginey's.

It was a precarious position to be in in her new high heels and she had to clench her calf muscles almost painfully to stop herself from falling ignominiously off the bed. Paul was pathetic in his excitement, staring up at her exposed sex like a slathering animal.

Anna did not bother to hide her revulsion.

Veering from her script, she laid into him verbally.

'God, Paul, you disgust me! Look at you, tethered like a dog, getting your jollies from the fear that I might beat you with this crop!'

'Oh yes, yes please, please beat me!'

'You're not listening to me! I don't want to play your sordid little games, you . . . you stupid little pervert!'

'Yes! Yes!'

Anna shook her head in disbelief as she saw how much her contempt was exciting him.

'I mean it, Paul. Really – I think you're pathetic!'

'I am, oh God, I am. I'm pathetic, not worthy to look at you – piss on me, Mistress, let me feel how much I disgust you!'

Anna stared at his once beloved face, contorted now in a rictus of warped ecstasy and she was sorely tempted to do just that. She *had* intended to lay about him with the crop, to mark him in some way, but now she couldn't be bothered. It came to her in a flash – the best, the most satisfying way to humiliate him.

Climbing carefully off the bed, she went over to the wardrobe and stripped off the restricting corset. She hadn't realised until that moment exactly what it was that she intended to do. Suddenly, everything fell into place. Dominic's invitation, Alan's heavy-handed hints that he would understand if she should suddenly decide to 'disappear' without notice.

She was already pulling on jeans and a T-shirt before Paul realised what she was doing.

'Anna?'

She turned and watched as, with the realisation

that the game was over, his penis slowly deflated. That was revenge enough for her.

'What are you doing?' he asked her, his voice rising in panic.

'I'm packing, darling – can't you see?'

'Packing . . . but – you can't!'

'Can't I?'

'Where are you going?'

Anna ignored him as she stuffed her passport and wallet into the bag.

'I'll send for the rest of my stuff later.'

'But . . . Anna wait! For God's sake!'

She stopped at the door, turning to him questioningly.

'You can't leave me like this!'

What he had clearly meant to be a reasonable appeal came out as a whine.

Anna smiled. 'But I thought that was what you enjoyed best, Paul. Humiliation.'

He spluttered, his voice rising on a note of hysteria as he realised she was serious.

'Anna, be reasonable! How am I supposed to get out of this?'

Anna blew him a kiss. She would ring one of his friends from the airport, but he didn't need to know that just yet.

'*Au revoir*, Paul. Or rather, *GOODBYE*!'

Picking up her holdall, she ran down the stairs, leaving him trussed, naked, to the bed.

To her surprise, she found Francine waiting for her outside in her car. Slipping into the passenger seat, Anna grinned at her.

'You knew I'd do it, didn't you?'

Frankie merely smiled, pulling an envelope

from the glove compartment and passing it to Anna as she switched on the engine. Inside was a ticket to Paris. A single ticket.

'What—?'

'Dominic asked me to get it for you. He'll be waiting at the airport.'

Anna felt excitement leap from her head to her toes. Was he so sure of her?

'There's just one thing,' Anna confessed as they drew up at the short-stay car park at Heathrow, 'I left Paul tied to the bed.'

'You did what?' Frankie began to laugh. 'Give me your keys,' she demanded.

'My keys?'

'I'll go and release him – eventually.'

Seeing the light of mischief in Francine's eyes, Anna laughed and handed over her door keys.

'Have fun!' she said as she hugged her friend goodbye.

'And you. Always fun.'

'Yes. *Au revoir*, Frankie. And thank you – for everything.'

'Don't mention it.'

The two women hugged again, then Anna climbed out of the car and walked quickly into the airport to find a plane which would fly her across the channel to a new life – and Dominic.

☐	Back in Charge	Mariah Greene	£4.99
☐	The Discipline of Pearls	Susan Swann	£4.99
☐	Hotel Aphrodisia	Dorothy Starr	£4.99

X Libris offers an eXciting range of quality titles which can be ordered from the following address:

Little, Brown and Company (UK),
P.O. Box 11,
Falmouth,
Cornwall TR10 9EN.

Alternatively you may fax your order to the above address. Fax No. 0326 376423.

Payments can be made as follows: cheque, postal order (payable to Little, Brown and Company) or by credit cards, Visa/Access. Do not send cash or currency. UK customers and B.F.P.O. please allow £1.00 for postage and packing for the first book, plus 50p for the second book, plus 30p for each additional book up to a maximum charge of £3.00 (7 books plus).

Overseas customers including Ireland, please allow £2.00 for the first book plus £1.00 for the second book, plus 50p for each additional book.

NAME (Block Letters) ....

....

ADDRESS ....

....

....

☐ I enclose my remittance for _____

☐ I wish to pay by Access/Visa Card

Number ☐☐☐☐☐☐☐☐☐☐☐☐☐☐☐☐

Card Expiry Date ☐☐☐☐